FOCUS ON THE FAMILY®
presents

HEART
to
HEART™

Stories
for
Teachers

compiled and edited by
JOE L. WHEELER

TYNDALE HOUSE PUBLISHERS, INC.,
WHEATON, ILLINOIS

Visit Tyndale's exciting Web site at www.tyndale.com

A Focus on the Family book published by Tyndale House Publishers, Inc.

Designed by Jenny Swanson

Woodcut illustrations are from the library of Joe L. Wheeler.

Published in association with the literary agency of Alive Communications, 7680 Goddard Street, Suite 200, Colorado Springs, CO 80920.

Scripture quotations are taken from the *Holy Bible,* King James Version.

Library of Congress Cataloging-in-Publication Data

Focus on the Family presents heart to heart stories for teachers / complied and edited by Joe L. Wheeler.
    p. cm.
ISBN 0-8423-5412-3 (hc)
1. Education—Fiction. 2. Teacher-student relationships—Fiction. 3. Christian fiction, American.
4. Short stories, American. 5. Teachers—Fiction. I. Title: Heart to heart stories for teachers.
II. Wheeler, Joe L., date. III. Focus on the Family (Organization)
  PS648.E33 F63 2003
  813′.0108355—dc21   200214488

Printed in Italy

08   07   06   05   04   03
6   5   4   3   2   1

Dedication

She not only brought me into the world, she introduced me to it.
She homeschooled me for fourteen of the first sixteen years of my life.
Before I could read she filled my memory bank with stories, poetry,
and readings. Almost never have I heard her misenunciate a word.
I was not yet five when I discovered the magic of print. I remember
yet how I relentlessly pursued her everywhere she went in our Long
Beach, California home, reading out loud to her book after book after
book. When I was eight, our family moved to Latin America. She
continued to teach me. More significantly, she gave me wings. Almost
every week we'd go to the American library and I would return home
with as many books as I could carry. Then I'd devour them: I'd hide
them under textbooks I was supposed to be studying, and I'd sur-
reptitiously read them by flashlight under the covers far into each night.
She encouraged me to explore every road I wished to follow.

She also taught my brother, Romayne (previously of Vienna, Austria;
now of Creel, Mexico), who has since become a world-renowned
pianist, composer, and poet. And she taught my sister, Marjorie
(of Red Bluff, California), who late in life has blossomed into an award-
winning artist. Besides us, she has taught hundreds of other children in
schools both in Latin America and North America. Whomever her life
touched, that person's life was never the same again.

Whatever I have since become, if indeed I am the Renaissance man
some accuse me of being, it is all her doing, that small, frail, but
indomitable woman I am proud to call both Mother and Teacher.

BARBARA LEININGER WHEELER

of

ROSEBERG, OREGON

CONTENTS

ACKNOWLEDGMENTS

Introduction: "What Is This Thing Called Teaching?" by Joseph Leininger Wheeler. Copyright © 2002. Printed by permission of the author.

"The Beginning," by Arthur Gordon. Reprinted by permission of Pamela Gordon.

"The Girl in the Fifth Row," by Leo Buscaglia. Published in *Reader's Digest,* February 1984. Reprinted by permission of The Felice Foundation and The Reader's Digest Association, Inc.

"All the Good Things," by Sister Helen Mrosia. Published in *Guideposts,* December 1999. Reprinted by permission of Guideposts, Inc.

"The Stuffed Kitten," by Mae Hurley Ashworth. Published in *The Town Journal,* December 1953. If anyone can provide knowledge of where the author (or author's next-of-kin) can be found, please send to Joe L. Wheeler (P.O. Box 1246, Conifer, CO 80433).

"Toughy," by Hiram Haydn. Published in *Reader's Digest,* June 1946. If anyone can provide knowledge of earliest publication or where the author (or author's next-of-kin) may be found, please send to Joe L. Wheeler (P.O. Box 1246, Conifer, CO 80433).

"The Golden Chain," by Josephine DeFord Terrill. Published in *The Youth's Instructor,* 1931, and in *Red Letter Day and Other Stories* (Hagerstown, Md.: Review and Herald Publishing Association, 1942). Text reprinted by permission of Joe L. Wheeler (P.O. Box 1246, Conifer, CO 80433) and Review and Herald Publishing Association, Hagerstown, MD.

"The Tiger," by Mary Dirlam. Published in *Practical English,* May 1953. Reprinted by permission of Scholastic, Inc.

"A Woman to Warm Your Heart By," by Dorothy Walworth. Originally published in *The Baltimore Sun,* March 5, 1944, and condensed by *Reader's Digest* in April 1944. Reprinted courtesy of *The Baltimore Sun* and with permission of The Reader's Digest Association, Inc.

"The Yellow Shirt," by Joan Marie Cook. Excerpted from *The Window Tree and Other Stories* (Hagerstown, Md.: Review and Herald Publishing Association, 1960). Reprinted by permission of the author.

ACKNOWLEDGMENTS

"A Little Brown Bulb," by Leeta McCully Cherry. Published in *The Youth's Instructor*, February 19, 1929. Text reprinted by permission of Joe L. Wheeler (P.O. Box 1246, Conifer, CO 80433) and Review and Herald Publishing Association, Hagerstown, MD.

"Mountains to Climb," by Russell Gordon Carter. Published in *Young People's Weekly*, September 30, 1934. Text reprinted by permission of Joe L. Wheeler (P.O. Box 1246, Conifer, CO 80433) and Cook Communications Ministries, Colorado Springs, CO.

"Number Nine Schoolhouse," author unknown. If anyone can provide knowledge of authorship and earliest publication, please send to Joe L. Wheeler (P.O. Box 1246, Conifer, CO 80433).

"Unloved, Unwanted, Until . . . ," by Lola Kovener. Published in *Guideposts*, February 1961. Reprinted by permission of Guideposts, Inc.

"Girls Will Be Girls," by Patricia Sherlock. Published in *Good Housekeeping*, March 1976. If anyone can provide knowledge of where the author (or the author's next-of-kin) may be found, please send to Joe L. Wheeler (P.O. Box 1246, Conifer, CO 80433).

"Matilda," by Mary E. Mitchell. Published in *The Youth's Instructor*, October 6, 1925. Text reprinted by permission of Joe L. Wheeler (P.O. Box 1246, Conifer, CO 80433) and Review and Herald Publishing Association, Hagerstown, MD.

"Father Flanagan's Toughest Customer," by Fulton Oursler, Jr. Published in *Reader's Digest*, February 1947. Reprinted by permission of Fulton and April Oursler and The Reader's Digest Association, Inc.

"A Lesson in Discipline," by Teresa Feley. If anyone can provide knowledge of earliest publication or where the author (or author's next-of-kin) may be found, please send to Joe L. Wheeler (P.O. Box 1246, Conifer, CO 80433).

"Bobbie Shaftoe," author unknown. Published in *The Youth's Instructor*, September 4, 1928. Text reprinted by permission of Joe L. Wheeler (P.O. Box 1246, Conifer, CO 80433) and Review and Herald Publishing Association, Hagerstown, MD.

"Research Man," by W. R. Van Meter. Published in *Young People's Weekly*, January 16, 1938. Text reprinted by permission of Joe L. Wheeler (P.O. Box 1246, Conifer, CO 80433) and Cook Communications Ministries, Colorado Springs, CO.

"The Boy Who Couldn't Be Saved," author unknown. If anyone can provide knowledge of authorship and earliest publication, please send to Joe L. Wheeler (P.O. Box 1246, Conifer, CO 80433).

Introduction

WHAT IS THIS THING
CALLED TEACHING?

Joseph Leininger Wheeler

The telephone rang . . . and our daughter's voice was on the line. After small talk we moved on to what was uppermost on her mind: how and when to begin educating their two boys, Taylor (four) and Seth (one). Should they consider preschool before kindergarten? There are so many options to consider: regular public school, charter schools, Christian schools, and homeschooling. Which ones would be worthy of their trust? When should they start Taylor? They certainly didn't want to shortchange him. Could he get quality education in Christian schools? Could he get the right kind of instruction in values at charter or public schools? All these questions spilled out pell-mell, one after another, in almost a torrent.

Later on that morning, I asked some young women in a dental office if they felt our daughter's concerns were typical of most young women. They nodded their heads and declared, "We *all* share her concerns. We've *all* worried about such decisions. How is a parent to know?"

One of the things I said to our daughter was this: "The single most important thing to look for is passion. Is the teacher passionate about learning and life?" Later on, thinking back to this collection of teacher stories, it came to me that this incredibly complex thing we label "education" is not nearly as forbidding as we tend to make it. If we cut through all the academic mumbo jumbo to the distilled essence, education is merely a caring teacher sharing his knowledge with a willing student. An old saying reiterates this definition of education:

> *A student seated on one end of the log,*
> *and Mark Hopkins[1] seated on the other.*

MY OWN JOURNEY

Several years into college, I began to stumble into the teaching profession. My parents were teachers, ergo I could become one too. Whatever I didn't yet know about teaching I'd learn in my education classes and in my student teaching.

Wrong.

Education classes could no more make a teacher of me than psychology books could show me how to fall in love. And student teaching didn't help either. My supervising teacher appar-

[1]*Famed American educator, 1802–1877*

ently did not know how to teach—or even to arouse enthusiasm in his pupils. No deader classes have I ever experienced.

About fifteen months later, the last student shut the classroom door and took his seat, the class bell rang, and I was face-to-face with this thing called teaching. I got by that first day by asking the students about themselves and their interests. And I told them about mine. Then I gave them an assignment.

But the next day came the moment of truth: In spite of all those years of college course work, I still did not know how to teach.

❧

It was years later before I fully realized that I was anything but alone in this feeling of unpreparedness. And it was many years more before I felt good about my teaching. Good—just that, no more—for, in teaching, one *never arrives*. It is the most inexact of all sciences, with the possible exception of parenting: Not until our children are grown do we learn what parenting is. Our first child proves very little, for each later child teaches us that what worked for one will not necessarily work for another. If we have five children, we are left at the end not with one well-proven philosophy of raising children—but with five.

The same is true with teaching.

So now, over forty years later (thirty-four of those in the classroom), I have a clearer picture of what it means to be a teacher. Let me share some of these hard-earned lessons and conclusions.

First of all, let's tackle two misperceptions about the educational process:

The first one has to do with testing, which supposedly will confirm my success or failure as a teacher. It didn't take long for me to have real doubts about this premise, for my students apparently had sieve-like brains and forgot what they had "learned" at a dismaying speed. But I was almost to the end of my teaching career before I learned the awful truth. The top information literacy specialist in America addressed our college faculty one never-to-be-forgotten day and asked us all this question: "Let's say you are giving a test tomorrow. One week from tomorrow, how much will your students remember of what they know tomorrow?" When she asked us to guess the answer, not one of us was even close! *The top student in your class will have forgotten a minimum of 82 percent by the end of that first week. The rest of the class will have forgotten even more. And it's all downhill from there.*

So we were confronted with the unthinkable: If what students "learn" cannot be retained for even one week, how do we evaluate the effectiveness of our teaching?

The second is one of the chief misperceptions in academia today. Simply put, it is the assumption that grade point average determines one's destiny. It supposedly reflects how well you will do in standardized testing, shows what caliber of college or university will accept you, and determines whether or not you will succeed outside the traditional classroom.

Bilgewater!

If this were true, why are so many homeschoolers being accepted by the most elite universities? Why are so many straight-A graduates working for C-plus bosses? Why do so many four-pointers have such difficulty relating to people? Belatedly, many discover that, while they may have mastered content regurgitation, by ignoring the opportunities for growth and leadership in student association, musical groups, clubs, publications, tutoring, study-travel abroad, service organizations, etc., their social skills failed to grow. Thus they never became what they could have been, and they missed out on making the deepest and longest-lasting friendships life brings us.

Not that high grades and effective study skills aren't desirable, for they are. And the mind ought to be so cultivated. Nevertheless, we must never forget that we ought to be educating the whole person, not just the ability to remember long enough to pass tests.

Even IQ is overrated. All too often it proves a liability to be so intelligent you can ace exams without bothering to study. Many of these brilliant ones coast so much of the time that they are intellectually flabby by the time they graduate. Never having had to struggle for anything, a surprisingly large number of them are passed up by the plodders. For success is not to be found in mere pyrotechnics but in long-term, day-in, day-out sustaining.

So it is that even students who earn mediocre grades have the potential to make a success of the rest of their lives. To rise, in fact, to the very pinnacle of human achievement. And students who excel in their classwork may also succeed in the real world if they will also develop their nonacademic talents, skills, and graces.

So what does all this mean in terms of the teaching profession?

Well, it means that we will have to look outside testing and grade point average for answers. As for myself, it was amazing how many answers I found in these stories of unforgettable teachers.

For one thing, it's obvious that early teacher evaluations mean little. Young people are no more capable of differentiating between a real teacher and a pseudo one than children are capable of judging how wise or effective their parents are. True wisdom comes only with the years, in the biblical "fullness of time." With the passing of the years comes a reevaluation of our teachers. While young, we give our kudos, adulation, and year-book dedications to those who please us most, cater to us, placate us, and smooth our paths. But the ones who care about us enough to be tough, to challenge, to expect nothing but our best, and are willing to wait for appreciation until the battering of the years re-sorts our priorities—these are the great ones.

UNFORGETTABLE

One of Nat King Cole's most beloved songs bears this title. What qualities are likely to make a teacher "unforgettable"? (In a good sense, that is. For it is said that "no one is ever completely useless—you can always serve as a horrible example.") Great teachers tend to be known for certain qualities, qualities each of us could develop if only we cared enough.

PASSION AND COMPETENCE

Almost never is a teacher fondly remembered who lacks enthusiasm and passion. A man or woman who is in love with life and learning is an exciting person to be around. It's almost impossible to avoid being infected by such a spirit. When compared to the instructor who merely does what he or she is paid to do (show up at scheduled classes and appointments, explain the subject matter, test, and grade), it is no contest. One has a force field, the other does not. One is the stuff of anecdotes and legend, the other of yawns and shaken watches.

I have never forgotten a statement I heard years ago at a teaching convention: "There is only one unforgivable sin in teaching—and that is to bore your students."

The speaker did not mean that teachers had to be slapstick comedians, but rather that they ought not only to be interesting to listen to but also to be known for substance. There is a principle at stake here: I can steal just as surely by snatching away a person's time as by stealing possessions. I cringe when I see a public speaker rambling. Not to be prepared, not to know what he is going to say, is a theft of our most priceless and irreplaceable possession—time. The same is true for teachers: *Every teacher* ought to err on the side of overpreparation, knowing ahead of time what she is going to say. How the class is to be kept interesting and meaningful, how it will help to prepare students for life itself. At the end of a given class, each student ought to feel that his tuition money was well spent and that he gained new insights into life.

Ironically, the only area I know of where people seem over-joyed at not getting their money's worth is education: "Miss a school day? Hooray! Teacher sick? Wonderful!" Nevertheless, a teacher who consistently shortchanges students will be remem-bered in later years—but not fondly.

Students ridicule teachers who are unprepared. They do not expect their teachers to know *all* the answers, but they expect competence. They will throng to the teacher who brings joy and excitement to each class. Laziness in teaching repels them. Stu-dents mock teachers who merely recycle class notes, lectures, and tests. Even fellow teachers soon learn which instructors are laughingstocks because students are collecting their old tests and getting A's without having to learn the material.

No teacher unworthy of respect will ever be considered great. Students are in full agreement with the old aphorism "What you are roars so loudly in my ears, I can't hear what you say."

Only when the walk and the talk are synchronized can there be respect. Students can smell a fake a mile off. And they deeply resent being pandered to.

FELLOW LEARNERS

Great teachers do not pontificate but rather consider themselves fellow learners. Oliver Wendell Holmes postulated that the teacher should not speak *at* students, from the front of the room, but rather *with* the students, facing the same direction they do.

Students love to study with teachers who are continually learning themselves. How well I remember Dr. Paul Quimby, an eminent scholar of Far East history. One of the part-time jobs I held in college was to wash pots and pans in the cafeteria each morning. When I went to work at 5 A.M., I could count on seeing a light on in Dr. Quimby's office. Even with his vast knowledge of his subject matter, he never considered it enough. What an inspiration that was for me as a fledgling history student! By example, he taught me that learning must be both continuous and lifelong. It is for this reason that all of my classes tend to be taught with the chairs arranged in a circle—this way no one is minimized or left out, and the teacher is on level, approachable ground, as a fellow learner.

LOVE

But having stirred in this characteristic and that, this quality and that, there remains one magical factor in the mix without which no teacher can ever achieve greatness. And that is, quite simply, *love*. Sooner or later, after all the nuts and bolts of teaching are sorted out, after the craft of teaching has been honed, there will come a time when the teacher must make a crucial decision: whether or not to really love each student. This is the toughest decision a teacher can ever make, for once it is made, life will never be the same. It is far, far easier just to patter on about content than to invest lifeblood in one's students. To take the trouble to *really* get to know each student—to search out the hidden dreams, the inner torment rarely revealed to anyone, the sources of joy and meaning—that is a tall order indeed!

It is impossible to fake love successfully. The eyes do not lie. If you are sincere, love will permeate every word you write, every look you give, everything you say, and thus each student will *know* that here is true love, as unconditional and permanent as the everlasting hills. It means being there for each student as long as life shall last. And each student will drain one's energy reserves, much as was true when Christ stopped in midjourney, turned around, and asked of the vast crowd of people who were jostling Him the seemingly ridiculous question, "Who touched Me?" Someone there wanted more than a mere touch, and Christ sensed that need instantly.

In today's litigious society, we have reached the point where it is dangerous even to touch another human being. Given the fact that each of us is said to need eight hugs a day in order to remain sane, not to touch, not to hug, is a recipe for disaster. I have always hugged. So has my family. I really don't know how I could effectively communicate love without it.

Teaching unstrengthened by the divine will inevitably fall short. Since God is the ultimate source of all true love, those who are not connected with Him will be little more than hollow drums. *With* that relationship with God, it won't be necessary to preach a creed; every word, every act, every glance, every nuance will give away the truth.

Second only to love, and a by-product of it, is *kindness,* perhaps the single most significant character trait in the universe. If a teacher is not kind, the best thing he or she can do is to flee the classroom and never darken its door again! And with kindness comes empathy, the key to understanding and relating to our students.

With love and kindness comes a willingness to mentor. It is said that we learn more from our mentors than from all of our textbooks combined. Mentoring relationships can be official or unofficial. Each day, people watch us and are impacted by what we say, write, or do—whether or not we're aware of it. But official, conscious mentoring is a higher art and can easily be abused. A true mentor will resist the devotee's tendency to idolize or clone and will instead search out and emphasize the mentoree's unique strengths and skills. A true mentor's motives will always be selfless, realizing that real success occurs only when the mentoree has moved on to self-sufficiency and has begun to mentor others.

You never know when your words will be transformed into life-changing epiphanies. Case in point: Back in the 1960s I was taking English classes, one at a time, at Sacramento State University. One particular day, as I was walking past my advisor's office, I was startled to hear him call out, "Joe! Got a minute?"

I answered in the affirmative, went in, and took a seat. After some small talk, he asked me a rather strange question: "Joe, what are you doing here?"

I sputtered that I was taking English classes.

"Why?"

"Oh, so I can complete my undergraduate major. I graduated with a major in history, but only a minor in English."

"Do you realize you're already halfway to a master's in English?"

I had not realized. Dr. Victor Comerchero's unsolicited question changed the course of my life, setting in motion events that propelled me out of secondary teaching and into the college level, laying the stage for my doctorate and for all the scholarship

that followed—all because he cared. Teachers have this power—
if they will but use it.

NEW BEGINNINGS

One serendipity about teaching is that each day you are given the
opportunity to make a new beginning. When I come home
burdened by the conviction that I failed in that day's classes, I can
determine that tomorrow's will be better. If a semester or a year
ends poorly, I can turn things around before I begin another.

The stories that follow offer each of us the opportunity to walk
in the footsteps of our protagonists. Beginning teachers can thus
avoid many mistakes, and veteran teachers can gain new insights
into qualities that make a teacher unforgettable.

In these stories we learn that it is not new buildings, comput-
ers, and state-of-the-art visual and audio equipment that result in
great teaching. Perhaps Frances Hungerford (in Walworth's story
"A Woman to Warm Your Heart By") put it best:

You see, all I had was love.

ABOUT THIS COLLECTION

Since I have been a teacher myself for thirty-four years, I have
taken great joy in including wonderful teacher stories in our
many story anthologies over the years. When my editor at
Tyndale asked me to put together a collection of the most
memorable teaching stories I had ever read, I started by making
copies of those I had anthologized over the years, then stirred
into the mix the best of those I had yet to include in a collection.
The final test came when I reread all of them, pretending I was
reading each one for the very first time. Which ones had the
most power? Which ones moved me most deeply? As a result,

twelve of my previously anthologized teacher stories made the cut, and twelve new ones displaced the others.

Featured in this collection are such luminaries as Arthur Gordon, Josephine DeFord Terrill, Dorothy Walworth, Fulton Oursler, Jr., and Russell Gordon Carter.

THE
BEGINNING

Arthur Gordon

Parents are our first teachers and the ones who care most about us. But sooner or later there comes a time when those first teachers must step aside. But even when they do, they agonize, wondering if they made the right decision.

*T*he September morning was calm and bright. The town looked fresh and shining and very American. We drove slowly through the gilded streets, not saying anything.

Sherry sat beside me, scrubbed and solemn. We had decided, her mother and I, not to make anything momentous of this first day at school. I was to drop her there and drive on. She knew which classroom was hers. We had all inspected it the week before.

Symbolically, perhaps, the school was on a hill. A flight of steps rose from the street, bisecting the green lawn, arrowing straight to the wide door centered in the red-brick Colonial building. A public school. A good one, so they said.

Already a trickle of small humanity was flowing up the steps. It was easy to spot the first-graders. Most of them were anchored to their mothers' hands. I glanced at Sherry. She was staring at her lap.

"We're a little early," I said. "Want to sit here for a couple of minutes?"

She nodded. I leaned forward and cut the ignition. I had not expected to feel anything, but now I felt a queer breathlessness, as if I were waiting for something important to happen.

Sherry smoothed her dress carefully over her knees. The part in her hair looked very straight and white. *What is she thinking?* I asked myself suddenly. *What goes on inside that bright, new, untouched mind? Does she know what it means, this first step on the endless ladder of education? Does she have any idea? Of course she doesn't,* I told myself impatiently. *If she did, she'd probably jump out of the car and run away. How many years of classrooms? Twelve, at least. Sixteen, if she goes to college. More, if she goes on to graduate school or gets specialized training.*

I gripped the wheel tighter, thinking of all the unknown

individuals who would try to teach this child and in trying would leave some mark, however tiny, on her mind or her heart. Frightening, somehow. Terrifying, almost.

Sherry lifted one foot and examined the scissor scratches on the sole of her new shoe. *They will explain the physical world to you,* I thought. *They may show you how to blueprint the atom. They may give you a map of the spiral nebulae. But who will help you know yourself? Who will teach you to chart your own emotions? Who will offer you a guide to the frail complexities of the human spirit? Nobody, nobody. . . .*

Try to learn their facts, I said to Sherry in my mind, *but don't worry too much if you can't. You'll forget most of them anyway, sooner or later. I memorized the quadratic formula once, and read all the plays of Molière in the original. What earthly good it did me I still don't know. The things that matter you won't learn from any blackboard. That I can promise you.*

A knot of small male animals went by, full of raucous high spirits. *There go your real teachers, Sherry,* I said to her silently. *Take a good look at them, your contemporaries. They will teach you many things that are not in any schoolbooks. Unpleasant things sometimes. How to lie, how to cheat, goodness knows what else. . . .*

Maybe you have to learn those things before you can also learn that ultimately they're not worth doing. I don't know. I'm your father, and you think I know everything, but you're wrong. All I really know is that I don't know much—and when you make that discovery about yourself someday, why then the first part of your education will be complete.

But they won't teach you that in school, either. If they did, much of the importance of what they're doing with all their chalk and books and rulers would melt away, and that would never do.

The happy savages went whooping up the steps. Sherry watched them, and I watched Sherry. *Five minutes from now,* I thought, *you won't be just you anymore. You'll also be one of them. It may be the biggest step you'll ever take. I hope it's in the right direction.*

I looked at the school high on the hill and the open door with the little figures going into it, and a clammy doubt seized me, a doubt as to the ultimate wisdom of pouring these young lives into such a mold, however good, however well intentioned. Conformity, regimentation, the desire not to be different but to be as much like everyone else as possible—was this *really* the way to develop independence, originality, leadership?

No such school system existed when our country was born. Yet consider the genius that blazed forth in those days. Washington, Jefferson, Franklin, Hamilton, John Marshall, Patrick Henry—all these and many more from a tiny nation of barely three million souls. Now we number 200 million, and schools and colleges cover the land. But where are the leaders, where are the men?

I glanced again at the child beside me. *Maybe it doesn't matter,* I thought. *Maybe the pattern is already set. Maybe the seeds of personality are already planted and nothing can alter the way they will grow. Maybe—I don't know. One more thing I don't know.*

Anyway, I said to myself, *the time has come. Open that tight parental hand and let her go. It's her life, remember, not yours.*

I reached across her and opened the door. She got out slowly and stood with her back to me, looking up at the building on the hill. Now I was supposed to drive nonchalantly away.

"So long, Sherry," I said.

She turned her head, and suddenly that wonderful flood of love and humor came up behind her eyes.

"Don't be scared, Daddy," she said. "I'll be back." And she went climbing up into the blue infinity of the morning.

Arthur Gordon
(1912–2002)

During his long and memorable career, Arthur Gordon edited such magazines as *Cosmopolitan, Good Housekeeping,* and *Guideposts.* He was the author of a number of books, including *Reprisal* (1950), *Norman Vincent Peale: Minister to Millions* (1958), *A Touch of Wonder* (1983), and *Return to Wonder* (1996), as well as several hundred short stories.

THE GIRL IN
THE FIFTH ROW

Leo Buscaglia

*P*erhaps it is because I, too, am a professor that this story hit me with such force. I, too, took far too many students for granted, passed up many an opportunity to affirm. It is so easy just to teach the material, prepare the student to pass your tests, and forget to search for the soul behind those two windows to the world: the eyes.

"[The circumstances of this story] changed my life," testified Buscaglia. Well, the story has changed my life, too. Never again have I been able to enter a classroom without trembling a little lest I, too, miss the *last* opportunity to affirm, to love. I have come to realize that unless I truly love my students—EACH of them, regardless of looks or personality— then I have no business in the classroom.

But what really scares me is the realization that so many other teachers have not yet realized or internalized this sad truth: to be neglected, unaffirmed at home; and neglected, unaffirmed at school . . . is a recipe for another Liani.

*O*n my first day as an assistant professor of education at the University of Southern California, I entered the classsroom with a great deal of anxiety. My large class responded to my awkward smile and brief greeting with silence. For a few moments I fussed with my notes. Then I started my lecture, stammering: no one seemed to be listening.

At that moment of panic I noticed in the fifth row a poised, attentive young woman in a summer dress. Her skin was tanned, her brown eyes were clear and alert, her hair was golden. Her animated expression and warm smile were an invitation for me to go on. When I'd say something, she would nod, or say, "Oh, yes!" and write it down. She emanated the comforting feeling that she cared about what I was trying so haltingly to say.

I began to speak directly to her, and my confidence and enthusiasm returned. After a while I risked looking about. The other students had begun listening and taking notes. This stunning young woman had pulled me through.

After class, I scanned the roll to find her name. Liani. Her papers, which I read over the subsequent weeks, were written with creativity, sensitivity and a delicate sense of humor.

I had asked all my students to visit my office during the

semester, and I awaited Liani's visit with special interest. I wanted to tell her how she had saved my first day and encourage her to develop her qualities of caring and awareness.

Liani never came. About five weeks into the semester, she missed two weeks of classes. I asked the students seated around her if they knew why. I was shocked to learn that they did not even know her *name*. I thought of Albert Schweitzer's poignant statement: "We are all so much together and yet we are all dying of loneliness."

I went to our dean of women. The moment I mentioned Liani's name, she winced. "Oh, I'm sorry, Leo," she said. "I thought you'd been told. . . ."

Liani had driven to Pacific Palisades, a lovely community near downtown Los Angeles where cliffs fall abruptly into the sea. There, shocked picnickers later reported, she jumped to her death.

Liani was twenty-two years old! And her God-given uniqueness was gone forever.

I called Liani's parents. From the tenderness with which Liani's mother spoke of her, I knew that she had been loved. But it was obvious to me that Liani had not *felt* loved.

"What are we doing?" I asked a colleague. "We're so busy teaching *things*. What's the value of teaching Liani to read, write, do arithmetic, if we taught her nothing of what she truly needed to know: how to live in joy, how to have a sense of personal worth and dignity?"

I decided to do something to help others who needed to feel loved. I would teach a *course* on love.

I spent months in library research but found little help. Almost all the books on love dealt with sex or romantic love. There was virtually nothing on love in general. But perhaps if I offered myself only as a facilitator, the students and I could teach one another and learn together. I called the course Love Class.

It took only one announcement to fill this non-credit course. I gave each student a reading list, but there were no assigned texts, no attendance requirements, no exams. We just shared our reading, our ideas, our experiences.

My premise is that love is learned. Our "teachers" are the loving people we encounter. If we find no models of love, then we grow up love-starved and unloving. The happy possibility, I told my students, is that love can be learned at any moment of our lives if we are willing to put in the time, the energy and the practice.

Few missed even one session of Love Class. I had to crowd the students closer together as they brought mothers, fathers, sisters, brothers, friends, husbands, wives—even grandparents. Scheduled to start at 7 P.M. and end at 10, the class often continued until well past midnight.

One of the first things I tried to get across was the importance of touching. "How many of you have hugged someone—other than a girlfriend, boyfriend or your spouse—within the past week?" Few hands went up. One student said, "I'm always afraid that my motives will be misinterpreted." From the nervous laughter, I could tell that many shared the young woman's feeling.

"Love has a need to be expressed physically," I responded. "I feel fortunate to have grown up in a passionate, hugging Italian family. I associate hugging with a more universal kind of love.

"But if you are afraid of being misunderstood, verbalize your feelings to the person you're hugging. And for people who are really uncomfortable about being embraced, a warm, two-handed handshake will satisfy the need to be touched."

We began to hug one another after each class. Eventually, hugging became a common greeting among class members on campus.

We never left Love Class without a plan to share love. Once we decided to thank our parents. This produced unforgettable responses.

One student, a varsity football player, was especially uncomfortable with the assignment. He felt love strongly, but he had difficulty expressing it. It took a great deal of courage and determination for him to walk into the living room, raise his dad from the chair, and hug him warmly. He said, "I love you, Dad," and kissed him. His father's eyes welled up with tears as he muttered, "I know. And I love you, too, Son." His father called me the next morning to say this had been one of the happiest moments of his life.

For another Love Class assignment we agreed to share something of ourselves without expectation of reward. Some students helped disabled children. Others assisted derelicts on Skid Row. Many volunteered to work on suicide hot lines, hoping to find the Lianis before it was too late.

I went with one of my students, Joel, to a nursing home not far from U.S.C. A number of aged people were lying in beds in old cotton gowns, staring at the ceiling. Joel looked around and then asked, "What should I do?" I said, "You see that woman over there? Go say hello."

He went over and said, "Uh, hello."

She looked at him suspiciously for a moment. "Are you a relative?"

"No."

"Good! Sit down, young man."

Oh, the things she told him! This woman knew so much about

love, pain, suffering. Even about approaching death, with which she had to make some kind of peace. But no one had cared about listening—until Joel. He started visiting her once a week. Soon that day began to be known as "Joel's Day." He would come and all the old people would gather.

Then the elderly woman asked her daughter to bring her a glamorous dressing gown. When Joel came for his visit, he found her sitting up in bed in a beautiful satin gown, her hair done up stylishly. She hadn't had her hair fixed in ages: why have your hair done if nobody really sees you? Before long, others in the ward were dressing up for Joel.

The years since I began Love Class have been the most exciting of my life. While attempting to open doors to love for others, I found that the doors were opening for me.

I ate in a greasy spoon in Arizona not long ago. When I ordered pork chops, somebody said, "You're crazy. Nobody eats pork chops in a place like this." But the chops were magnificent.

"I'd like to meet the chef," I said to the waitress.

We walked back to the kitchen, and there he was, a big, sweaty man. "What's the matter?" he demanded.

"Nothing. Those pork chops were just fantastic."

He looked at me as though I was out of my mind. Obviously it was hard for him to receive a compliment. Then he said warmly, "Would you like another?"

Isn't that beautiful? Had I not *learned* how to be loving, I would have thought nice things about the chef's pork chops but probably wouldn't have told him—just as I had failed to tell Liani how much she had helped me that first day in class. That's one of the things love is: sharing joy with people.

Another secret of love is knowing that you are yourself special, that in all the world there is only one of you. If I had a magic wand and a single wish, I would wave the wand over everybody and have each individual say, and believe, "I like me, right this minute. Just as I am, and what I can become. I'm great."

The pursuit of love has made a wonder of *my* life. But what would my existence have been like had I never known Liani? Would I still be stammering out subject matter at students, year after year, with little concern about the vulnerable human beings behind the masks? Who can tell? Liani presented me with the challenge and I took it up! It has made all the difference.

I wish Liani were here today. I would hold her in my arms and say, "Many people have helped me learn about love, but you gave me the impetus. Thank you. I love you." But I believe my love for Liani has, in some mysterious way, already reached her.

Leo Buscaglia
(1924–1998)

Leo Buscaglia, alias "Dr. Hug," was one of the most beloved figures in America. The Associated Press obituary began, "Self-help author Leo Buscaglia, the bearded, teddy-bear-like apostle of love who customarily ended his motivational speeches by giving everyone in the audience a hug. . . ." Buscaglia wrote more than a dozen books that sold more than 11 million copies and were translated into twenty languages. Two of the best-known are *Loving Each Other* and *Living, Loving and Learning*.

ALL THE
GOOD THINGS

Sister Helen Mrosia

When she took a break from algebra and gave her class an unusual assignment, she had no idea what a powerful thing she was setting in motion.

*I*t was 1959. I'd been assigned a third-grade class at Saint Mary's School in Morris, Minnesota. I loved my students, especially Mark. He was polite to a fault, always said please and thank you, and held doors open for other students. But, like any child his age, he tested the limits. Once, when I sent him to the cloakroom for punishment, he climbed through the window and up the fire escape to the roof. Sometimes he wouldn't stop talking. He didn't do it to be rude; he just couldn't help himself. Still, I couldn't stay upset with him for long. Whenever I corrected him for misbehaving, he thanked me. And he bubbled with so much happiness and energy that just looking at him made me smile.

That year of teaching wasn't always fun. Maintaining control of the classroom was exhausting, and it was made worse when I lost my voice for thirty-five days. I learned to get the children's attention by enunciating clearly. If that didn't work, I fell back on a glare my students dubbed Look Number 13. That quieted them, even Mark. Usually.

Novice teachers make mistakes, though, and I made one of my biggest with Mark. One day, despite my repeated warnings and his good intentions, nothing could get him to keep quiet during the reading lesson. My patience wore thin. I looked at Mark and said, "If you say one more word, I am going to tape your mouth shut." I never thought I'd have to follow through on my threat, but not ten seconds later another student blurted, "Sister, Mark is talking again."

I worried my students wouldn't respect my authority if I didn't do something, so I walked to my desk, very deliberately opened a drawer and pulled out a roll of masking tape. Without saying a word, I went to where Mark was sitting, tore off two pieces of tape and used them to make a big X over his mouth. Back at the front of the class, I glanced up from the reading book to look at Mark. He winked at me. That did it. I started laughing. The class laughed too. Shrugging, I went back to Mark and removed the tape while the rest of the class cheered. Ever polite, he said, "Thank you for correcting me, Sister."

That's how I learned not to threaten or embarrass a student in front of others. Ever.

The following year I was transferred to junior-high-school math. Five years later Mark turned up in my eighth-grade class. He was as engaging as ever and had learned not to talk so much. Math was a tough subject, though, for him and the rest of the students. One Friday, after a long week of struggling with prealgebra, I could tell they were frustrated. An idea came to me. I'd always written personal comments on students' papers before I handed them back, perhaps because I still appreciated the only such note I had ever received (a nun once wrote "Thank God for the good grade" on an A+ paper of mine). Now I wondered what the students thought about one another. That led to a spur-of-the-moment assignment.

I asked my students to put away their textbooks, take out some blank paper, and list the names of their classmates, leaving a line of space between each name. Then I told them to write down the nicest thing they could think of about each person.

It took the rest of the period for them to finish. I wrote my own list while they worked on theirs. It was so fun to watch them. I could tell who they were writing about because they'd lift their heads and look at a classmate for inspiration. Then their faces would light up and they'd scribble something down and turn to the next student.

That weekend I compiled the lists for each student, transcribing the comments and adding my own at the end. I imagined how delighted each person would be after reading the good things others had to say.

On Monday I handed back the lists. Soon the entire class was smiling. "I never knew that meant anything to anyone," I heard one student whisper. "I didn't know people liked me so much," said another.

None of them ever mentioned it again. But the exercise had accomplished what I'd hoped it would—they were happy with themselves and their classmates, and ready to learn.

The school year ended and Mark moved on. I became friendly with his family, and after he finished high school we exchanged letters. He wrote to me from Vietnam, where he'd been assigned to the 585th Transportation Company in Phu Bai, delivering supplies to fire bases. His letters told me how scared he was of all the shooting and death around him. He had horrible nightmares. I said I was praying for him daily and shared stories about my current class.

When I returned from a summer vacation in August 1971 my parents met me at the airport. As we were driving home my mother asked me the usual questions about my trip. There was a lull in the conversation. Mother gave Dad a sideways glance and he cleared his throat, as he usually did before saying something important.

"The Eklunds called last night," he began. "Mark died in Vietnam. The funeral is tomorrow. They'd like it if you would attend." I can still point out the exact spot on I-894 where Dad broke the news.

The church was packed with mourners. I was last in the long line that filed past Mark's coffin. All I could think was, *Mark, I'd give all the masking tape in the world just to hear you talk again.* Then, at the cemetery, a young soldier approached me. "Were you

Mark's math teacher?" he asked. I nodded, and he said, "Mark talked about you a lot."

After the funeral there was a reception at a farmhouse nearby. Mark's parents came up to me. "We want to show you something," Mr. Eklund said, taking a wallet out of his pocket. "They found this on Mark. We thought you might recognize it." He opened the billfold and removed a worn piece of paper that had been unfolded and refolded countless times. I knew without even looking that it was the list of good things Mark's eighth-grade classmates had said about him.

"Thank you for doing that," Mrs. Eklund said. "Mark treasured it."

A group of Mark's former classmates gathered around us, peeking at the list. Charlie smiled sheepishly and said, "I still have my list. It's in the top drawer of my desk at home."

Chuck's wife said, "Chuck asked me to put his in our wedding album."

"I have mine too," said Marilyn. "It's in my diary."

Then Vicki reached into her pocketbook, pulled out her wallet and showed her frazzled list. "I carry this with me everywhere," she said. "I think we all saved our lists."

That's when I sat down and cried.

Words of encouragement are important; even more valuable is what I learned from Mark. I was a novice teacher in those days, struggling to teach third grade. There I found that God puts students in my classroom not only so they can learn, but also so I can learn. Today—teaching college—I look back to Mark as one of my greatest teachers. That impish boy with his nonstop chatter and winning smile taught me to accept people for who they are—a lesson I sorely needed and one I try to pass on to all my students. It's the best way I can think of to celebrate Mark's life.

Sister Helen Mrosia

Sister Helen Mrosia wrote for magazines during the second half
of the twentieth century.

TOUGHY

Hiram Haydn

$\mathcal{N}$obody likes principals. Or learns anything from them. But . . . somebody forgot to tell Toughy that.

*E*verybody called him Toughy. One boy's parents had been away during the three months since the youngster entered Toughy's school, and when they came to see this place the boy introduced them proudly to members of the faculty. "This is Mr. Watson, this is Miss Graham, and this is our principal, Mr. —Toughy." His face was crimson; he couldn't remember the principal's name, for he hadn't heard it since the opening day of school.

To the three of us who were new to teaching, Toughy's influence over the pupils in this private school for boys was incomprehensible. We could not understand how he could control them by "talks." He never seemed to have a disciplinary problem, while we had so far taught nothing but discipline. And even with so limited a program, I, for one, had not achieved notable success. At the end of the first three months I picked up bodily one fresh little boy and carried him into Toughy's office.

"Take him," I said, "before I murder him." It was my intention to resign that evening. But a half hour later this boy came back to class so quiet, so polite, so cooperative, that I changed my mind. When I asked Toughy what had happened he replied, his eyes twinkling, "We had a talk."

His authority was so quiet that we seldom had a chance to observe just how he got his results. But at last I asked him quite bluntly.

"The first rule," he said, "is not to allow a crisis to develop. It's much harder to control a situation satisfactorily if it has reached the stage that calls for punishment. Never put a boy in the position where he can challenge or defy your instructions and where, if he says the wrong thing, you'll have to call his bluff. Never ask him if he's done something wrong when you feel sure he has, for you're tempting him to lie his way out of trouble."

That was clear and concrete, and it made sense. "But I still can't fathom," I said, "how you can always see trouble brewing."

"You have to know your boy," Toughy replied. "It's always there to see, long before it actually comes on. A tantrum doesn't come without any warning from a well-adjusted boy. And with a small school, we have a real chance to know our boys."

Toughy required us to make a report every six weeks on each of ten or twelve boys, giving an estimate of each one's character—his initiative, adaptability, trustworthiness, and other qualities. If, after reading a character report, parents of boys who needed correction were too indifferent to see where the finger pointed, Toughy would let them know, tactfully but honestly, what imminent trouble was brewing, and what they could do to help to avoid it. The resulting teamwork among boys, teachers, and parents was remarkable.

Every noon some committees of boys met at lunch with Toughy or a teacher to plan programs or activities. One, called the Executive Committee, was really a cover name for Toughy's Trouble-Shooters. No other award in school meant so much as membership on that committee. Once on it, you were on the inside; you were working with Toughy to see to it that every boy was getting the encouragement and opportunity he needed to find himself. No member of the committee ever broke the trust invested in him: to keep secret the problems discussed there.

Of course Toughy was not "tough." On the contrary, he was the gentlest man I have ever known. But it was the sort of gentleness that comes from genuine strength. He made terrific demands on himself and on everyone else. For he expected everyone at the school to live up to his full capacity; he asked that you find your best self and keep constant pace with it.

At first glance, there seemed nothing remarkable about him.

Of less than average height, trim, intelligent-looking, his only unusual feature was a patch of white in his early-graying hair. But as you saw more of him, you became increasingly aware of the warmth and humor in his eyes, of the power of the well-shaped hands that were never restless or emphatic, and of the richness of his deep voice. By the time you had been working with him a year you wondered why such a man was content to stay on as principal of a struggling little school conducted in a frame house. For you were sure he could have his pick of any principal's job. And, too, you wondered where he had come from—in a deeper sense than the merely geographical. He talked little of himself, but I gradually pieced the story together.

When Henry Mortimer returned from France and was discharged from the Army in 1919 he headed for art school. From boyhood days his fingers had itched for a drawing pencil and paintbrush. Now, in his late twenties, at last he had the money and the chance to get the training he wanted.

For six months he studied in Chicago. It was clear to his teachers that this man had a brilliant artistic career before him. When he went back to Rochester to visit his parents during the spring holidays, he was bubbling with enthusiasm for his work.

On the way back he stopped in Cleveland to see his uncle, who had started a boys' school. It was an impulsive decision; its effect lasted a lifetime.

He found the new school sadly crippled. One of the teaching staff of four persons had left for another job. A second teacher had just gone to the hospital—out for the rest of the school year.

His uncle, trying to do the work of three men, was obviously worn out.

Henry looked around him. There was something in the air in this little school that was arresting and exciting. It was apparent in the two remaining teachers; it was vividly alive in the boys (they didn't feel the way he had about school—they almost had to be forced to go home at the end of the day); and it shone from his uncle's eyes.

He realized suddenly that he was breathing the same creative air he had found at art school. Only here the tools were not pencil and brush, but mind and heart; the medium was not paint and canvas, but human lives.

"You're tired out," he said to his uncle. "Let me take your classes this afternoon. They may not learn much geography, but I think we'll get along."

They got along. And that night at his uncle's apartment he said abruptly, "If you'll take me, I'm staying."

It was not so easy as that. For weeks there were times when he yearned to get to the easel, when he felt that he had made a bad mistake. But the weeks grew into months, the months into years. And when at a dinner party one night he met a girl with laughing blue Irish eyes, the decision became irrevocable.

He married Helen Gallagher, and by the time I arrived at the school their baby boy was six months old. They were living in a small house near the school, which had thrived sufficiently to warrant moving it out into a suburb where there were open fields and country air. His uncle had retired, and Henry Mortimer had charge of the Lower School (grades one through six). Henry Mortimer had become Toughy.

Slowly I began to understand the principles behind Toughy's success with boys. In the first place he loved boys, unashamedly and wholeheartedly. And since he loved them, he believed in them. I have seen him take on, with quiet confidence, boys of whom parents, friends, even child psychiatrists had despaired. "They haven't been handled right," he would say.

But he would hit the right combination. If Bill Graham was lazy and irresponsible, Toughy would heap responsibility on him. For instance, he would leave the next "town meeting" in Bill's hands and walk off as though there were no question about its working out satisfactorily. If Dan Billings was a buffoon whom everybody ridiculed, Toughy would call him in and ask him to serve as chairman of the Reception Committee, whose function was to escort guests around the school.

Sometimes, of course, along would come a particularly hard customer who would tax even Toughy's efforts. One was ten-year-old Douglas Hall, whose father had died while Douglas was a baby and whose mother had granted him his every whim. Douglas was devoid of physical fear and of social responsibility. Once while he was roughhousing, his arm went through a windowpane and was ripped open from elbow to wrist. Ignoring the blood spurting from the jagged wound, he walked over to me and calmly said, "I guess something ought to be done about this."

Knowing that ordinary methods wouldn't work with Douglas, for a long time Toughy did nothing but cement a bond of friendship with the boy. He found out and shared Douglas's interests; he overlooked offenses that he would usually have dealt with severely.

We couldn't see that Toughy was making great headway, but we had to admit that Douglas liked and respected him as he did no one else. So matters went for several months. Then came a showdown. Douglas began to feel his oats too much and bullied other boys openly. It looked as though Toughy were finally going to fail.

But one day I met Douglas coming down the hall crying. I stared. *Douglas crying!* It took me ten minutes to persuade him to tell me the cause, but he finally did. "I got kicked out of class," he blubbered, "and sent up to Toughy. And he told me he—he was disappointed in me. He said no good friend would let a friend down—the way I did."

The crisis had been passed triumphantly, after a long campaign. And I suddenly caught a glimpse of how heroic Toughy's patience was.

When I met Toughy an hour later and saw how tired and drawn he was, I suddenly realized how completely and exhaustingly he threw himself into this precarious business of reshaping young lives.

Toughy's love of and belief in boys were matched only by his love of and belief in the sheer excitement of the learning process. This was evident in all his classes. Under this guidance, fifth- and sixth-grade geography and history took on the romantic glamour that boys usually found only in interplanetary comic books and the kind of radio programs to which parents object.

Toughy taught early American history, for example, by making each boy in the class the governor of one of the original colonies. For several weeks each student would, with Toughy's help, gather information about his colony. He would find the school library inadequate, and would spend Saturdays at the public library. He would *live* in 17th century Massachusetts or Virginia or Rhode Island.

Then would come the roundup. In a classroom electric with excitement, each boy had to answer in detail any pertinent questions about his colony that the other boys and Toughy could think up—and they could think up some devilish ones. I remember how a ten-year-old governor of Connecticut stood on one occasion for forty minutes, giving out answer after answer about crops, Indian attacks, government. Completely at ease across the reach of 250 years, he would always begin, "Well, this is the way we handled that—"

Part of Toughy's magic formula unfolded itself in those classes. Consciously or unconsciously, all of us who teach or have taught want the almost impossible combination of being at one with our students—at home with their idiom, at ease in their world—and yet of not sinking to their level of immaturity and thus relinquishing the guiding hand that steers their activities. All good teachers approach this precarious balance; Toughy is the only one I have ever seen who maintained it without a slip of any kind. In the history game, he was one of them in a completely easy and natural give-and-take, as excited and eager as any of the students. Yet he had only to say, "Are you sure about that, Dan?" and a thoughtful and attentive silence would come over the group.

Geography games were the order of the day at lunch, and so engrossing that competitors would frequently forget to ask for a second dessert. One year some youngsters gave up afternoon play periods for months to construct a large cement relief map of North America in the schoolyard. Only an extraordinarily dull boy emerged from a year or two of Toughy's geography classes without a Quiz Kid's knowledge of boundaries, natural resources, and topography.

If we tried to compliment Toughy on his teaching, he would merely reply, "Thanks. Say, have you noticed what a great job Dave is doing in teaching his general science class?" or "Isn't that a first-rate idea of Gil's to have the kids decorate the library with illustrations from their favorite books?" Eventually, of course, Dave or Gil would tell the rest of us where the "great job" or the "first-rate idea" had originated—in a conference with Toughy.

Toughy's enthusiasm for the job was contagious; it spread through the faculty. We became restless when away from the school; we began to come back after supper, to plan and discuss. As a result, informal faculty meetings would be held night after night in which we discussed boys, methods, and projects.

The men on that faculty are scattered now, but we haven't forgotten Toughy any more than the old boys have. He did as much for us as for the boys. In teaching us how to know and draw the best out of boys, he also taught us how to know and draw the best out of ourselves.

Toughy had many tempting offers to head other schools at higher salaries. When I asked him why he had turned one such offer down, he looked embarrassed.

"Why, I can't leave here," he said, as close to angry as I can remember. "This is where I belong."

So he did. He meant, first of all, that he felt he had a personal obligation to his uncle. This would always be his school, in a way that no other could be. But what he said was true in a more general sense, too. Anybody belongs where he has found that he can utilize his powers to the fullest, where he can make every day exciting and enriching for himself and the people he works with.

If I've written of him as though his career were over, it's

because for me every thought of him is so clearly tied up with the days of the school in the little frame house. Actually, the school has expanded and is still going, and Toughy is still the principal of its elementary grades. He was offered the principalship of the whole school but turned it down. "I work best with younger boys," he said.

The frame house is gone; the younger boys are now housed in a big red-brick building with the older ones. The enrollment has increased; the staff is larger. Everything has changed—except Toughy.

The last time I saw him I tried to get him to tell me how he liked the changes in the school, and whether he was still happy at his old job in its new surroundings. But he wouldn't talk about himself.

"Say," he exclaimed, and the old light shone in his eyes, "I want you to meet Dick Price, the new manual-training teacher. He's got the boys working on a great Christmas project. He has some wonderful ideas!"

Hiram Haydn

Hiram Haydn was born in Cleveland, Ohio. He was editor of *American Scholar,* editor in chief at Random House, president of Atheneum Publishers, and co-publisher of Harcourt, Brace and Jovanovich. Besides this he wrote books such as *By Nature Free* (1943), *Manhattan Furlough* (1945), *The Time Is Noon* (1948), *The Counter-Renaissance* (1950), and *The Hands of Esau* (1962).

THE GOLDEN CHAIN

Josephine De Ford Terrill

As always, the freshmen were lonely and homesick. But what could one person do about such a perennial college problem?

hyllis sat down on the long oak bench that stood across the end of the hall near the letter rack just outside the Dean of Women's door. The handwriting on her letter aroused her curiosity; she must read it before she went down to supper. It read:

Dear Phyllis:

You have been chosen from the group of girls in college this year to become a member of a club which is being formed at this time. Until we can have our first meeting to discuss the details more fully, we think it would be better if the existence of the club is unknown to the general student body.

Phyllis flipped the page over to find the signature. Margaret Eman, the lovable psychology teacher! Her eyes shone with excitement as she devoured the rest of the letter.

In the meantime, we have outlined some definite work to be done by the members. The requirements for this week are to be as follows:

First, please memorize these words: "I expect to pass through this life but once. If, therefore, there be any kindness I can show, or any good thing I can do to any fellow being, let me do it now, and not defer or neglect it, as I shall not pass this way again."

Second, please find time for a short get-acquainted conversation with ten freshman girls, and keep a list of their names where no one will see it. Your purse will make a perfect hiding place.

If you feel that you do not care to join our club, please see me in my classroom not later than tomorrow afternoon. Otherwise we

shall consider you one of us. Remember, we shall depend upon you not to discuss this letter or the plans of the club with anyone.
   Be diligent! Be true!

Very sincerely yours,
Margaret Eman

Phyllis read the letter through twice before she thrust it into her pocket and went down to supper. A sudden elation filled her. The words were tingling in her brain: "*You* have been chosen." "A club which is being formed." Was she being rewarded for some unremembered act of friendliness, to be chosen from among all the girls at Wilbur College? Hardly knowing what she was doing, she chose her tray of food at the cafeteria counter and walked into the dining room. There was a scattering of students there. Two freshman girls were sitting alone at a table over in one corner. Instantly Phyllis realized that here was her first opportunity to begin work for the club.

"Do you mind if I sit with you?" she asked, her voice vibrant with emotion.

The girls looked up in surprise and murmured something in unison, while Phyllis removed the food from her tray and sat down.

"I hope I'm not interrupting a private chat," she began.

"Not at all," assured one of the girls.

"We just stick together because we don't know anybody else," giggled the other.

Phyllis smiled. "Are you roommates?"

"Yes, we are," replied the first student, her voice warm and courteous.

"Is this your first year?" A useless but complimentary remark.

"Yes, we're freshmen," laughed the second one again.

Phyllis liked them both at once, the one with her infectious sense of humor and the other whose manners were so lovely. They ate in silence for a moment, then a question was asked, and Phyllis soon found herself expanding garrulously, her new interest in philanthropy luring her on. She told them useful details of dining-room procedure to which both girls listened eagerly. After they had finished eating, Phyllis asked if they would like to walk around the campus as everyone did while waiting for the bell to call them in to worship. The girls readily agreed. As they passed groups of wistful-eyed freshmen, Phyllis imagined that they looked enviously at the two of their number who had grown so chummy with a sophomore.

As soon as worship was over, Phyllis hurried to her room and, snatching a piece of paper, wrote two names and thrust them into her purse.

After breakfast the next morning, before her seven-thirty class began, Phyllis saw a girl standing beside the banister on the first floor of the administration building. Hildreth was one figure in the freshman class who could not fail to attract attention, for she was probably the tallest person in the entire school. Phyllis sauntered down the stairs and stopped two steps from the bottom, which put her on a level with the girl's face. "We are both early birds," she remarked, to open the conversation.

Relieved by the sense of ease which it gave her to be on a level with the one to whom she was speaking, Hildreth smiled, her finely wrought face lighting up eagerly. "Then we should be lucky all day," she answered, her voice low and very musical.

Something in the girl's face touched Phyllis' heart. *If there be any kindness I can show*—Surely these first days in a new place must be hard for a girl as conspicuous as Hildreth, for there is always the inevitable joker whose lack of heart matches his lack of wit, always new faces to stare at with faintly concealed amusement. Seeing the fine edge of defiance in the girl's eyes, Phyllis resolved suddenly that she would come here a little early every morning to stand on the steps and talk with her.

"What class are you waiting for?" she asked.

"I'm taking psychology from Miss Eman."

"Isn't she marvelous?" exclaimed Phyllis.

"I think she is very charming and unusually capable as a teacher."

"Everyone adores her. I had her last year."

"Are you a junior?"

"No, a sophomore."

When Phyllis went to her room for a moment just before chapel, she did not forget to slip a new name into her purse, and with a heart pounding with joy, she repeated the already special verse: "I expect to pass through this life but once. If, therefore—"

Every day Phyllis watched her mailbox for a letter announcing the meeting of the new club. Exactly one week from the day the first letter came, another lay in her compartment of the letter rack. Eagerly she opened it.

> *Dear Club Member:*
>
> *By now you have begun to understand the meaning and the purpose of our organization. I want to thank you for the way you have responded to the work asked of you. Already we seem to have achieved our aim, which is: 'Not a lonely girl in Wilbur College.'*
>
> *That corroding loneliness which destroys the happiness of the usual freshman's first weeks in school is not so evident this year, thanks to the work of our society. A friend with a smile and a*

cheery greeting is worth more at the beginning of the year than any number of friends at the end of the year. Those girls whom you have befriended this week will never forget you. I know because I was once a college freshman.

We find that we must postpone our meeting until a little later, but in the meantime, we want you to continue getting acquainted with freshman girls. Keep your list as you did last week. And please learn these words: "Happiness is a perfume which you cannot give to others without spilling a few drops upon yourself."

If you should feel the urge to discuss our club with one of your friends, turn to Matthew Six and read the first six verses.

Be diligent! Be true!

Sincerely yours,
Margaret Eman

At the end of the third week, the third letter came.

Dear Club Member:

We have decided to postpone our meeting until you have had an opportunity to meet every girl in the Freshman Class. So do not grow weary of well-doing.

Have you found the friend you have always dreamed of finding someday? Perhaps she is a member of this year's Freshman Class.

Somewhere there waiteth in this world of ours,
For one lone soul, another lonely soul;
Each chasing each through all the weary hours,
And meeting strangely at one sudden goal.

I shall write you each week.
Be diligent! Be true!

Sincerely yours,
Margaret Eman

Phyllis had little time any more for her own special friends, and though she missed them, the happiness she found in making new friends eclipsed the pleasure she had known in her old group.

She began to feel that she knew everyone in school, and she was constantly busy waving or smiling greetings as she went about her daily schedule. At the end of six weeks she had the name of every girl in the freshman class in her purse. Only a very few of them had not responded to her offers to friendship, but she determined to undermine their misanthropic tendencies bit by bit as the year progressed.

She knew that she had given happiness to many; yet she realized that she herself had received more than any of them. Her own ability to offer and accept friendship had increased a thousandfold, her powers of sympathy and understanding had deepened beyond measure, her poise and manner had gained in grace. The "spilled drops" of the perfume of happiness which had fallen to her made her feel that she must be the happiest girl in all Wilbur College. She often wondered which of the other girls were members of the society, but there was no evidence of a planned campaign of friendship, except, perhaps, the entire lack of cliques and the unusual intermingling of freshmen and sophomores.

A week before the Christmas holidays, a special meeting of the sophomore class was called in the chapel one evening after worship. A short business session was conducted first, and the boys were dismissed to return to their rooms for their evening study period. The faculty adviser made a few remarks and then turned the girls over to the special speaker, the psychology teacher, Miss Eman.

"We have come here for a double purpose tonight, girls," she began, her eyes smiling in their personal way. "I hope you won't feel that we have played too many tricks on you when we explain."

A faint suspicion began to brew in Phyllis's mind. She leaned forward in her seat.

"Last fall, your Dean and I decided to form a club comprising certain sophomore girls. We wrote you letters asking that you join and perform certain duties, which you have done wholeheartedly. I think that all the members of that club are here tonight, so we are going to reveal ourselves. Will those girls who belong to this club please stand?"

There was a moment of hesitancy as if the girls were reluctant to disclose Miss Eman's partiality. Then, here and there, the shuffling of seats. A moment of breath-taking silence. Then a storm of laughter broke out, and wave after wave swept back and forth across the chapel. Every girl in the room was on her feet!

When the laughter had subsided, the teacher spoke: "I was sure you would be surprised to learn that our club consists of the entire class. I simply could not decide which of you to leave out, so I chose every one of you. But I was afraid that if you knew that you were working as a class, you would not feel that same enthusiasm as if you worked independently."

Phyllis nodded her head, realizing the truth in that.

"I should like to tell you," began Miss Eman, composing her features for a long, serious talk, "just what started the idea of our club. Last fall, as I sat in chapel watching the freshman girls take their places for their first assembly, I wondered how many of them were suffering from homesickness. In spite of all that is done during the first days of school by the Dean of Women, the administration, the teachers, and the older students, we still find way too much real distress among our new students.

"So I began to study the situation and decided that if we had an organization the specific duty of which was to make friends with these girls, we could prevent much of this homesickness. We all realize that there is no particular character-building value in the agony of loneliness. It is true that we need to learn independence, to stand on our own feet, to know the value of solitude, but all these things can be learned much better when the mind is free.

"Out of the slough of loneliness sometimes grow rare and beautiful characters, but more often that slough produces only blighted and bitter personalities. In most cases here in school that early depression passes away with the finding of friends, but in the meantime there is much needless heartache. Far too often friendships are not formed until near the end of the year, whereas had they been made at the beginning, much happiness and benefit might have been realized.

"This year, by the help of my faithful crew of sophomore girls, we have had less homesickness than in any other year I have ever known. Innumerable fine friendships have formed already. School spirit and general co-operation have improved unbelievably."

As the tears gathered in her eyes, Phyllis knew the taste of real happiness. She recalled her struggles with Doreen, who at first was so unresponsive, so uncaring. Pauline had been contemptuous of the simple ways of their school; Harriet had not understood why rules must be obeyed.

Miss Eman continued: "The first week of school I talked

personally with every one of the freshman girls. The second week
I found time for a moment with every sophomore girl. I asked
many of them how they felt this year in comparison to the way
they felt at that time last year. Their answers convinced me that
among them I should find the helpers we needed. We teach
many subjects here in Wilbur College, but to me the most important thing to learn is the art of being kind. And to be kind in
this case means to be friendly. There was a little book published
a few years ago titled, *The New Thing in Her Heart*. It was the
story of a secret which an elderly woman whispered into the ear
of a young girl. The secret was this: *Everybody is lonesome!* If we
could always remember that, I am sure that we should always
be kind."

There was a sudden trembling in the speaker's voice. She
paused a moment. Then she said: "Let us repeat our first memory
verse in unison."

Slowly, with subdued emotion, they began: "I expect to pass
through this life but once. If, therefore, there be any kindness I
can show, or any good thing I can do to any fellow being, let me
do it now, and not defer or neglect it, as I shall not pass this way
again."

"Now our aim."

"Not a lonely girl in Wilbur College!"

"Our motto."

"Kindness is the golden chain by which society is held
together."

"Thank you, girls. And now may I tell you how much we
appreciate your work this fall. The faculty of Wilbur College is
proud of its class of sophomore girls. You have solved many
problems for us, and you have prevented many more problems
from developing. We shall always be grateful to you. And now

that you have done your work so well, we feel that there is no longer a need for our society to continue. Our first meeting is also our last. I am sure that each of you has learned enough about the joy of making friends to lead you to continue this delightful hobby throughout your entire life. You will always remember that we pass our way but once. Opportunities lost do not come again."

There was a moment's pause; then she continued: "Our experiment this year has been abundantly successful. Whether we shall try it again next year, we do not know. For the present, our work is done. Shall we feel free now to discuss our society and its methods? I shall leave that to the personal judgment of each girl. It seems to me, however, that we shall realize a more lingering satisfaction if we do not publish it abroad—at least until this present year is over. We do not want our freshman sisters," she laughed, "to think that we have gained their friendship by the aid of conspiracy.

"I believe that it is time now to return to your study period. Shall we stand and repeat for the first and last time, in unison, the last verse we learned?"

The girls rose, and with hushed voices repeated: "Make it a rule, and pray God to help you keep it, never to lie down at night without being able to say: 'I have made one human being a little wiser, or a little happier, or at least a little better, this day.' "

Margaret Eman's eyes were shining. "And now may I say 'Good night' to the grandest group of sophomore girls in any college in the world?"

Josephine DeFord Terrill

Josephine DeFord Terrill was a well-known writer of Judeo-Christian stories during the first third of the twentieth century.

THE YELLOW
SHIRT

Joan-Marie Cook

$\mathcal{T}$*he movie* Forrest Gump *brought home the concept that even those saddled with low IQ are worthy of being treated with kindness and consideration. This is just such a story.*

So this was my first college history class. The instructor walked in. He wore a shockingly yellow shirt and sat on the edge of his desk. He did not do our textbook the courtesy of opening it; instead he spoke to us, the students, of ourselves. He laughed often, and I thought I had never heard such a loud, uninhibited laugh. Professor Jackson's laugh amazed me almost as much as did his shirt.

History, to me, had always seemed to be too much involved with wars. A war, a war, and a war—with nothing in between but causes and effects. I was not prepared to enjoy a course in history.

Then, in the second week of the course, Professor Jackson assigned seats. Not alphabetically, but according to some secret scheme of his own, he lined us up by the blackboards and assembled us into rows. On one side of me was Nola Jeraldine Kirby, from "up in the mountains, close to Higginsburg," she told me. And on the other side, in immaculate white bucks and hand-knitted argyles, sat Thomas Webb Carpenter. I knew this, *not* because he ever spoke to me to tell me, but because that was the name I saw on his neatly folded papers on their way to the aisle. I knew about his shoes because I was too awed by him for days to really turn and look at him, but I could see his shoes by moving just my eyes. After all, his entrance exams carried marks that had made him quite well known on our campus. He was a brilliant boy.

The history class was more than I had guessed a class could be—a constant interplay of ideas, an occasional jab of debate, enough joking so that everyone in the room felt quite at ease. Professor Jackson was one of those rare teachers who could allow this great amount of freedom in a class without ever losing his control over the situation or his dignity. I began to treasure the professor's cogent beginning-of-class prayers, his reverent examination of history in relation to the Bible. His whole *feeling* for history crept in around the edges of my thinking. After a while I rather liked his laugh; there was something free and unafraid in the heartiness, the very loudness of it. And the yellow shirt—well, he hadn't many others, so I learned to face it with a resignation that approached bravery.

The professor assigned a great deal of outside reading and more outside projects than most of us thought were necessary. My project partners—Nola and Mr. Carpenter of the immaculate bucks.

Meanwhile, Nola, to my left, struggled valiantly to condense the swift discussions into notes with her leaking, scratching pen and her cheap cardboard notebook. And to my right, Thomas Webb Carpenter wrote his notes in flawless outline form without effort, without interrupting his own participation in a debate. Poor Nola, slow enough in any class competition, seemed even more painfully gross when compared with my other neighbor. I sometimes wondered if he ever saw her, noticed the way her plain, lonely face never changed from its strange, puzzled expression.

Sometimes when the topic was especially involved Nola would glance at my notes and sigh. It was such a tiny, helpless sigh, and if I whispered, "Never mind, Nola, you just listen today and I'll help you with your notes tonight," how she would smile at me.

We were in the library working on some map project, and I remember that the three of us were talking about what we would do after college. We were finished except for Nola, who was carefully coloring in a sea. Tom was telling us about his plans to become an engineer. His mother had insisted that he come to this college for at least a year, although he assured us he had no desire for the poverty connected with Christian service. Nola's hand, covered with small cuts and burns and stains from hours of work in the school kitchen, released its diligent grip on the crayon as she told us about the one-room building near her home where she wanted to start a school. "The church folks—they's all mighty anxious to help me get my two years' teacher training— no school a'tall for miles and miles up there. And the poor little children beyond Higginsburg, they don't have half a chance for growing up and meeting the world.

"I want 'em to have a real schoolroom like the one I got to go to when I stayed with my Aunt Jo, with real blackboards and a high shelf in the back to put their little lunch buckets on." She paused, her face flushed from so much unaccustomed talking. "I know you think I wouldn't be much of a teacher, because I'm not even what they call college material, but I'm all they got up beyond Higginsburg—and I love the children. Besides—" she leaned forward and her face took on an intensity that surprised me, "—besides, the Lord helps me to remember just the things I need to know. Just ask my orientation teacher; it's supposed to be impossible for anyone with an IQ as low as mine to make grades as good as I do. The Lord just knows my purpose and helps me. I study very hard, but I couldn't make it without the Lord."

I had never heard anyone speak so honestly about her limitations before, and I was stunned. There was no joking in her manner, nor sullenness; she merely stated the facts. Even Tom Carpenter was disarmed. He looked at her for a long moment and then he grinned and he said, "You'll make it, Nola. You really will. It's the spirit quotient that matters more than the intelligence quotient, and you'd rank genius there."

A dim smile crossed Nola's face. "The Lord helps me in all

sorts of ways," she repeated simply. Then she picked up the blue crayon and went back to work.

The next day in class I saw Tom watching Nola as she took her pitiful notes. It was the first time I had seen him really observe anyone else. The next class period I noticed something strange at the desk to my right. Tom was bent over his notes, writing longer sentences, taking time with his words. When the closing bell rang, I saw him remove a carbon and give the extra copy to Nola. He only spoke to her for a moment, but somehow I couldn't linger to hear their conversation. During the weeks to follow, the extra set of notes became a regular procedure.

We all became such special friends—Tom, Nola, and I. One day when Nola made the highest score on a daily quiz we all three nearly had to be sent from the room for laughing when, as we compared papers, Nola said, "I'm sorry, Tom. I'll help you study your notes next time."

Every week Tom and I made a special trip to the library to find outside reading that wouldn't be too hard for Nola. And together the three of us studied for all major history exams, although it must have been a trial for Tom. (He seemed actually to enjoy it.) And Nola, when she worked behind the counter in the cafeteria, saw to it that the largest desserts were saved for Tom and me.

Sometimes I wondered how much of this odd three-way part-nership had been planned in the secret mind of Professor Jackson, who never seemed to notice what his seating arrangement brought about.

Tom and I talked of the professor once. Tom said, "Isn't it just beautiful the way that brilliant man brings his vast energies to focus in a classroom? His methods are subtle, but if you observe closely—he knows every person in each class very well. The questions he asks each one are the questions that person needs to answer or think about. I wonder how he does it."

"Why don't you ask him?" I ventured.

"Perhaps I will." There was silence for a long while, and each of us returned to his homework. Suddenly Tom said, "But I could never be a teacher. How could one live on that kind of salary?"

The idea of Tom Carpenter as a teacher left me speechless for a moment. "I don't know, Tom, about living on the salary. I suppose you'd just have to believe the way Jackson believes, that self-denial and happiness go together in a Christian's life."

"That's the answer, of course." And he took up his trig problems again.

January came with long, gray days of monotony. Semester exams were just behind us; no vacation in sight, too early for picnics, banquets, et cetera, to begin. January seemed the ebb tide of the school year. One evening Nola called me to her room after study period. She stood in front of the mirror trying to appear absorbed in making her hair stay in pin curls. "I want you to pray with me tonight because the business manager called me to his office today. I guess I have to go home on account of I can't work any harder than I am now and I owe too much money."

"There must be some scholarship fund—"

"Not with grades like mine," and she shoved her report card at me. Straight Cs except for a D in a math subject.

"I'll talk to him, Nola; I'll think of something. You just can't go home now when you're so near through."

She was crying now, and something in the quietness of her soft sobs, the rigid way she stood there, with the tears washing down her pale cheeks, showed how confused and afraid she was.

"Someone used to help me," she finally said. "I don't know

who it was, but all last year and some this year, when things got pretty rough, someone would put some money in for me—sometimes just ten dollars, sometimes even fifty dollars. But this time, well, I just don't see any way out."

In my own room later I thought of Nola's progress—how painfully she had struggled with her grammar, how diligently she had studied her Bible lessons. What a beautiful lesson of faith she had been to me, for, just as she said, the Lord did know her purpose and did help her. Psychologists say that when it is difficult for a person to learn, it will usually be difficult for him to retain knowledge. This was not so in Nola's case. She remembered remarkably well. She constantly amazed her teachers. Then I began to wonder who had previously put money on her account. She didn't have many friends. Yet it must be someone who knew her fairly well, for who would put money to the credit of such a seemingly useless case unless he knew of her determination and dependence upon God?

The next day as I walked down a hall in the ad building, Professor Jackson walked out of the business office and joined me. There was a small slip of paper in his hand, which without notice he pushed into one of the books in the stack he was carrying. "I have something to tell you," he said, excitement sparkling in his eyes. "I just helped Tom Carpenter with his second semester schedule."

"He's changing his major?" I asked.

"I thought you'd like to know," he said, unable to stop smiling. "I was never so pleased as when he came and told me. He's taking a double major—history and education."

I was as happy as the professor had expected. On the sidewalk when we said good-by, he suddenly remembered a book he had for me. "Let's see, it's somewhere in this stack. I thought you might enjoy it for some outside reading," he explained, handing me a slim red volume of history in a period that particularly fascinated me.

In my room, when I opened the book, a small piece of paper fluttered to my desk. It was a receipt bearing that day's date. On it was written, "Paid to the account of Nola Jeraldine Kirby, one hundred dollars."[2]

It was weeks later in class one day that Nola whispered to me, "You know, I like that yellow shirt Professor Jackson has on."

I think she did not understand why there were tears in my eyes when I nodded my head and answered, "I think it's the nicest shirt I ever saw."

Joan Marie Cook

Joan Marie Cook, author of *The Window Tree and Other Stories* as well as a number of short stories, lives and writes today from Texarkana, Texas.

[2] *About $1,000 in today's money.*

THE STUFFED
KITTEN

Mae Hurley Ashworth

No story ever written better portrays the plight of the unlovely in the classroom. As for this one, the young teacher didn't really reject the little girl, she merely endured her attentions and her touch.

But how was she to know how little time she had?

*E*ach year at Christmas time, I set out upon the mantel a little old shabby, stuffed toy kitten. It's good for laughs among my friends. They don't know, you see, that the kitten is a kind of memorial—to a child who taught me the true meaning and spirit of giving.

The stuffed kitten came into my life when I was quite young and teaching third grade. It was the day before the Christmas holidays, and at the last recess I was unwrapping the gifts the children had brought me. The day was cold and rainy; so the boys and girls had remained indoors, and they crowded around my desk to watch.

I opened the packages with appropriate exclamations of gratitude over lacy handkerchiefs, pink powder puffs, candy boxes, and other familiar Christmas tributes to teacher.

Finally the last gift had been admired, and the children began drifting away. I started to work on plans for an after-holidays project.

When I looked up again, only one child remained at the table looking at the gifts. She did not touch anything. Her arms were stiff at her sides; but her head bent forward a little, so that the thick, jagged locks of her dust-colored hair hung over her eyes.

Poor Agnes, I thought. She looked like a small, dazzled sheep dog.

I had always felt a little guilty about Agnes because, no matter how hard I tried, I couldn't help being annoyed by her. She was neither pretty nor winsome, and her stupidity in class was exhausting.

Most of all, her unrestrained affection offended me. She had a habit of twining her soiled little fingers around my hand, or patting my arm, or fingering my dress. Of course I never actually pushed her away. Dutifully, I endured her love.

"Well, Agnes?" I said now. Abruptly she walked back to her seat, but a moment later I found her beside me again—clutching a toy stuffed kitten.

The kitten's skin was dismal yellow rayon, and its eyes were bright red beads. Agnes thrust it toward me in an agony of emotion. "It's for you," she whispered. "I couldn't buy you anything."

Her face was alive as I had never seen it before. Her eyes, usually dull, were shining. Under the sallowness of her skin spread a faint tinge of pink.

I felt dismayed. Not only did the kitten hold no charms for me, but I sensed that it was Agnes' own new and treasured possession—probably about the only Christmas she'd have.

So I said, "Oh, no, Agnes, you keep it for yourself!"

The shine fled from her eyes, and her shoulders drooped. "You—don't you like this kitten?"

I put on my heartiest manner. "Of course I like it, Agnes. If you are sure you want me to have it, why thank you!"

She set the kitten on its ill-made, wobbly legs, atop my desk. And the look on her face—I'll never forget it—was one of abject gratitude.

That afternoon, when the children were preparing to go home, Agnes detached herself from the line at the lockers and came over to my desk. She pushed her moist little hand into mine and whispered, "I'm glad you like the kitten. You *do* like it, don't you?"

I could sense her reaching out for warmth and approval, and I tried to rise to the occasion. "It's quite the nicest desk ornament I've ever had. Now run along, Agnes." I remembered to add, "And have a merry Christmas."

I watched the children as they marched out and scattered.

Agnes started alone down the walk, the rain pelting her bare head.

She was never to return to school. On her way home, a reckless driver ended the small life that had gone almost unnoticed in our community. . . .

On Christmas Day, I went to my deserted schoolroom to face the stuffed kitten—and to have it out with my own sick conscience.

Confession is healing, and I felt better after I had poured out my remorse to Agnes' mute gift. The giver was gone, beyond reach of the love and encouragement she had so desperately needed, and that I could have given her.

Or could I have—without Agnes' gift, and without her tragedy? Sometimes the capacity for responding to another's need comes only when the soul is *forced* to expand.

From now on, I promised the stuffed kitten, I would make children my life, not just my living. Besides teaching them the facts found in books, I would look into their hearts with love and with understanding. I'd give them myself, as well as my knowledge.

And heaven help me if I should ever again recoil from a grubby, seeking hand!

Mae Hurley Ashworth

Nothing is known today of Mae Hurley Ashworth.

A WOMAN TO WARM
YOUR HEART BY

Dorothy Walworth

The reporter wondered just what there was about this one very small teacher that changed so many lives. So she decided to find out.

*J*n Cornwall, an old Hudson River town at the foot of Storm King Mountain, a story began fifty years ago and has not yet ended. When I visited there last winter, the older people of the town told me about it. It is a story they are proud to remember. "She is a woman to warm your heart by," they told me. "And as for him . . ."

That September, when it all started, Cornwall's 70 eighth grade and high school pupils sat in a schoolroom only big enough for 20, waiting for a new teacher from upstate—an old maid in her thirties named Frances Irene Hungerford.

One of the high school students was Steve Pigott, a tall, lanky seventeen-year-old. Steve was good at his studies, but his father didn't see what use school was. He kept telling Steve, "You're old enough to cut out that foolishness." Pat Pigott was an Irish immigrant farmer who couldn't read or write.

Everyone was nice to Steve, but there was a difference, and he knew it. This was his second year in high school and he figured it would be his last. When the other boys talked about how they were going to make something of themselves, Steve never said a word.

Miss Hungerford turned out to be so small that when Steve stretched out his arm she could stand under it. But she stood straight as a footrule; she had steady deep-blue eyes, and when you looked into them you knew that all the winds over Storm King wouldn't budge her an inch. Her voice was pitched low, and her smile was like turning up a lamp.

One of the first things Miss Hungerford did was to write a sentence on the blackboard: "Seest thou a man diligent in his business? He shall stand before kings."[3] The schoolroom

[3]*Proverbs 22:29*

smothered giggles over that: as if anybody in Cornwall was ever going to get anywhere near a king!

In a week she had the high school wrapped around her little finger. If some of the boys had deviltry up their sleeves, she'd just smile, and her smile took the tuck right out of them. Every morning, at assembly, the eighth grade and high school sang. Steve had a fine voice, and so did Miss Hungerford, and the songs got to be like duets between those two, with the other pupils piping away in the background.

After assembly, classes began. There weren't enough seats to go around, so Miss Hungerford always gave somebody her chair and stood up all day. She taught every subject: French, German, algebra, history, English. She always gave her pupils the feeling that she learned with them. "Tell me about the Battle of Lake Erie," she'd say. "I'm curious to know."

Miss Hungerford started the Hawthorne and the Whittier literary clubs, where the boys and girls talked about authors and had ice cream afterward. Sometimes, during refreshments, she would talk about etiquette. She would say, "Now, Stephen Pigott, suppose you were invited to a formal dinner. How would you greet your hostess?"

"She's a *dedicated* sort of woman," people said, watching her walk back and forth from her boardinghouse to the school, early and late, in a shirtwaist and skirt and a little stiff hat, always with a load of books on her arm. She went to church twice on Sundays and to prayer meeting Wednesday nights. But she never said a word about religion, except for that sentence on the blackboard. She just sort of lived it.

Everyone has wondered since just what there was about Miss Hungerford that fired up her pupils so. Somehow she made them believe they lived in a fine world, where a miracle could happen any morning, and they were fortunate and wonderful, with a lot of talent. "We've never thought so well of ourselves since," the Cornwall people say. And she sent out from that school a batch of youngsters who became important men and women all over the country.

Miss Hungerford took trouble with everybody, but she worked hardest with Steve. He stayed on in high school. She told him over and over that books were important; they were doors. Steve began wondering if there might be a door for him. Especially the spring of his senior year, when they were reading "The Vision of Sir Launfal."

"A vision is a dream," Miss Hungerford told him, one night after school while he was clapping chalk dust out of the blackboard erasers. "My dream is always to stay with boys and girls and books. What is yours, Stephen?"

He said to her then what he'd never said to a living soul: "I want to be—a marine engineer."

He thought she'd laugh, but she sat there with her eyes sparkling. "You *can* be a marine engineer," she said. "All you need is the will to do it."

She had to give him faith in himself little by little. When she finally got Steve to speak to his father about going to college, Pat Pigott said Steve was crazy. Miss Hungerford was stubborn, though, and when fall came Steve went to Columbia University to take the mechanical engineering course.

He earned his way by working in a trolley barn; he sang in a church choir for five dollars a Sunday, and did all sorts of odd jobs, studying whenever he could. Every time he got to thinking he ought to give the whole thing up, he'd slip away to Cornwall and Miss Hungerford would somehow pour courage into him.

Stephen Pigott was president of the class in his junior year; he edited the engineering-school publication; he sang in the university glee club; he was elected to a Greek-letter fraternity. And when he was graduated in 1903, Miss Hungerford sent him a telegram: *I told you so.*

In 1908 Steve went to Scotland to help install a Curtis turbine for John Brown & Company, Ltd., the big shipbuilding firm that built the *Mauritania* and the *Lusitania*. He had planned to remain only four months, but the company persuaded him to stay on.

In 1938 he became managing director of the company. He had designed the machinery for more than 300 British ships: cruisers, submarines, the *Hood,* the *Duke of York,* the *Queen Mary.*

During these thirty years Steve and Miss Hungerford kept up their friendship, writing to each other almost every week.

On the *Queen Mary's* maiden voyage Steve came back to America for a few days. Columbia was giving him an honorary degree; the American Society of Mechanical Engineers was awarding him a medal.

When he went to Cornwall the whole town turned out to meet him; and he made a speech in the big new high school. Everyone expected him to talk about his work, or the fine people he had met abroad. But what he talked about was Miss Hungerford.

"Few men have been blessed with a friendship such as she has given to me for nearly half a century," he said. "When I have felt pride in any accomplished work, the things she said to me have been in my heart."

Miss Hungerford was now teaching in an upstate town near the shore of Lake Ontario. When Steve telephoned to say that he was coming to see her, he was told she was seriously ill, and was advised not to make the visit. And so he had to sail without seeing her.

Steve is Sir Stephen Pigott now—he was knighted in 1939, about the time he designed the machinery for the *Queen Elizabeth.*

Miss Hungerford, now eighty-five, is still living in her upstate town, where she had kept on working until she was almost eighty. A few years ago, her town dedicated to her the Frances Irene Hungerford Library, "in appreciation of her fineness of character, her devotion to her work, and the lasting impression she has made."

❧

That was the story they told me in Cornwall. It made me wonder what it was about Miss Hungerford that had made people remember her all their lives. So, a few weeks ago, I went upstate to spend a day with her.

She came running down the front steps to meet me, light as a feather. Her hair is snow white, but her eyes are the same deep blue. Even after what the Cornwall people had told me, I was not prepared for how tiny she is. Or how radiantly alive.

Her home is like her: tiny, cheerful, neat as a new pin. She showed me all over it, moving with quick, firm steps like a girl. In the book-filled sitting room I sat in her Boston rocker while she talked to me about Sir Stephen. She had newspaper clippings, pictures, Christmas cards, fifty years of his letters.

But, though I tried all day, I couldn't get Miss Hungerford to talk about herself. She was willing to tell only about her old pupils, calling each one by name. We had high tea at her grandmother's fine old table, and she asked a blessing. We spoke of how Sir Stephen had promised to come to see her when the war is over, of how he had written in his last letter: "Wait for me, Miss Hungerford."

"I hope," she said, "that I can live long enough to see Stephen again."

"Why, Miss Hungerford," I said, "you'll live forever!"

"I know that," she answered gravely, "but I may soon be out of touch with all you people for a little while."

When the car came for me, we walked to the curb together, her hand laid lightly on my arm. And then, for the first time, she spoke about herself. "You know, I feel ashamed," she said, "when I see all these bright modern teachers. Compared to them, I was not very well trained."

She paused; her hand tightened on my arm. "You see, all I had was *love.*"

Dorothy Walworth
(1900–1953)

Dorothy Walworth of Cornwall, New York, wrote such books as *Faith of Our Fathers, The Pride of the Town, Chickens Come Home to Roost, Rainbow at Noon,* and *Nicodemus.*

THE TIGER

Mary Dirlam

Teachers, like all mortals, yearn to be appreciated, liked, and loved. Yet it is the nature of the business they are in that they sometimes have to choose between popularity and its opposite, knowing deep down that an ounce of long-term respect and appreciation is worth a ton of short-term popularity.

Occasionally, during the swift-flying years, our lives are enriched by mentors with tough love, teachers willing to be misunderstood in order that the student is not

wrecked on the shoals of premature adulation or egocentricity.
Mark Spencer found that out too late.

*I*t seemed to Mark Spencer that in this room, at this moment, he had reached a pausing point. One phase of his life was over; another was about to begin.

His artist's eye took in the element of design in his immediate surroundings. There, sitting across the desk from him, was Dean Harber—all angles this man, with his wiry, energetic body. Through the window were the familiar outlines of the Bryant Art School buildings, which had been Mark's home for the past four years. On Harber's desk was the large rectangular folder marked "Spencer."

Harber leafed idly through the folder before he spoke. Then he looked up to smile at the young man who sat opposite him. "Well, here we are, Mark," he said. "You're through with us now—it's time. You've learned what we could teach you here. The rest will be work, experience, development."

"I know," Mark murmured. He watched in a detached way as the dean continued to leaf through his paintings. These papers and canvases were his achievements, the products of all the years during which he had known he was going to become an artist.

Dean Harber pulled out a watercolor from the folder and nodded in response. "Yes," he said. "You'll make the grade. They'll recognize you slowly—the artists first, then the critics. Sooner or later the public will catch on, too."

"Why are you looking at that landscape?" Mark questioned. "It's one of my high school things. A bad job."

"It has faults," Harber replied. "Labored—muddy. Yet there's something in it, too. Your high school work has always interested me, you know. It has ever since that day when your first folder came into my office." He put the watercolor down and fell into a reminiscent mood. "That folder—'Mark Spencer, Fairview High School, age seventeen.' We had hundreds of high school folders that year. But yours had something different about it. Yours showed development, the ability to learn—to go from good to better. Do you know what else it showed?"

"No," said Mark. "What else?"

"A teacher. I've always wanted to ask you about that teacher. Whoever he was, he knew what you could do and how to get it out of you."

"Old Greenbaum," Mark said softly, "Thomas J. Greenbaum. But—"

"But what?" asked Harber.

"I don't know what I was going to say exactly," Mark laughed. "Except that Greenbaum, my high school art teacher, wasn't the kind of man you seem to think he was. He was a tiger. I really hated him. He always had it in for me, you see. He was fairly decent with most of the others, but everything I did was wrong. Whenever I tried to meet him halfway, he'd always lash back at me with some sarcastic remark—putting me in my place. It always seemed as though he tried to be as unpleasant as he could."

Mark paused, staring at the watercolor which Harber had taken out of his folder. It was indeed a bad job—clumsy, uncertain; but he hadn't thought so at the time. It had taken Mark years to learn how to criticize his own work. Back in high school, every painting he'd done had seemed special and wonderful to him—even this watercolor.

Mark remembered the day in June, four years ago, when he had put this same watercolor into the folder that was going to

Bryant Art School. It had been just the day before commencement, and classes at Fairview had already ended for the school year. Mark, all his thoughts bent on his urgent desire to win the Bryant four-year scholarship, had come into the school art studio to assemble the last of the paintings and drawings that he would submit to Bryant as examples of his work. He had been holding the watercolor admiringly before him, pleased as he always was with what he had done, when Old Greenbaum entered the room.

"I am sorry," Greenbaum commented acidly, "to interrupt this touching scene between the artist and his work. I hope I don't intrude."

Mark flushed, putting the watercolor down on the table. Old Tiger Greenbaum and his poisonous tongue. Well, he wasn't going to have to put up with it much longer.

Greenbaum walked over to the painting and looked at it critically. "All blobbed up," he said dryly. "I wonder if you'll ever get over thinking that watercolor is oil paint."

"Listen, Mr. Greenbaum," Mark began, "I—"

Greenbaum interrupted as though Mark had not spoken. His gnarled index finger traced a line over the painting. "From there to there," he said in his rasping, metallic voice, "it's messy, undecided. Over here," he observed, pointing to another section, "the color looks as if it had been scrubbed with a wash brush." He seemed to hesitate for a moment. "The tree," he added grudgingly, "the tree is good."

Mark tried to swallow down his anger, as he had so many times before in the course of that year. He had bitten his lips and said nothing on all those occasions when Greenbaum had made him do sketch after sketch of the same subject—refusing to admit, even when Mark was certain that what he had done was flawless, that it could not be done better. He had worked in silent rage on difficult projects in perspective which he had no desire to attempt but which Greenbaum had insisted that he do. He had, more times than he could remember, resisted the temptation to throw his brush or charcoal stick in Greenbaum's face.

It had been necessary, Mark thought, that he should control his ever-mounting resentment of this inflexible, unsympathetic teacher. He couldn't afford to "tell him off" and to drop his course in art. For Mark knew, and had never questioned, that he must become a painter. That meant he must go to art school, and to go to art school, his high school record must be as superior as he could make it. There would be no art school for him without a scholarship—and no scholarship without real accomplishment in his high school art courses.

But now the school year was over. Whatever Old Greenbaum had had to say about Mark had already been said on the little blank which Bryant Art School sent to the teachers of scholarship candidates. And Mark was bitterly certain that Greenbaum's recommendation had been, at best, a halfhearted one.

He grabbed his watercolor from the table, where Greenbaum was standing before it. "I'm afraid I'm not interested in the rest of your criticism, Mr. Greenbaum," he said heatedly. "We're parting company now, and I can't say I'm sorry. You've never liked me—I don't know why, and I don't care any more. It goes without saying that I haven't liked you much, either. If I hadn't known, if I hadn't been sure, that I'm good, you would have discouraged me from ever going on with art. Maybe that's what you were trying to do, but I—"

Greenbaum, his face impassive, broke in on the angry boy before him. "But you never questioned your talent. We both know that. You've always been certain of yourself, of your paintings. In your own opinion, you could do no wrong."

"Come off it!" Mark retorted, forgetting in his emotion that he was talking to a teacher. "You must have known, even if you wouldn't admit it, that I'm as good a student as you've had at Fairview. You were standing right here, in this room, when Gustav Scholl told us both that I was one of the most promising students he'd seen in this country."

Gustav Scholl was a distinguished German painter who had visited Fairview High School earlier in the year, at Greenbaum's invitation. At the time, Greenbaum had unbent enough to make a special point of showing Mark's work to Scholl, and Scholl's reaction had been one of glowing enthusiasm. "My friend," he'd said, grabbing Greenbaum's arm in excitement, "this young man will do fine things!"

Now Mr. Greenbaum's lips pulled into a tight line as he said, "Ah, yes, our exuberant friend Scholl! His mistimed admiration did you a wrong, I think. He gave you that much more reason to believe in your own superiority."

Mark stuffed the last of his paintings into his folder. "And that," he replied, "is more than you've ever done for me. A complete stranger walking into this studio for a few minutes— and he gave me more encouragement than you've given me in a whole year. I could add," he said bitingly, "that Scholl's name means a good bit more in the world of art than your own."

A shadow of pain passed over Greenbaum's face, before he smiled the odd, stiff smile that Mark had come to know and mistrust. But he made no answer, and Mark took advantage of the pause to pick up his folder and leave the room.

Once out in the bright June sunshine, walking for the last time down the path that led from the art studio to the main building of Fairview High School, Mark experienced a twinge of regret. Maybe he shouldn't have been so rough on Greenbaum. There was no longer any point in nursing the grievances that had built up during the past year. Still, he couldn't believe that he had been unfair. Perhaps he'd even done some good. Greenbaum might think over what Mark had said to him and might recognize the justice of it.

Actually, Mark admitted to himself, Greenbaum was all right with the usual run of students. Most of the boys and girls at Fairview liked him. He was patient and gentle with the pupil who could hardly handle a brush, always encouraging to the awkward student who showed scattered signs of improvement. Why had he chosen Mark as his particular victim? Mark could only believe that it was jealousy—jealousy at discovering a teenager who already had more ability than Greenbaum himself possessed at the age of fifty-eight. . . .

It had all been so long ago—not long as years go, but long in experience. Now, sitting in Dean Harber's office, Mark found it hard to remember all the details of that year before he had been awarded the scholarship to Bryant Art School. At Bryant he had worked hard, won three major prizes, even sold one or two of his oil paintings. When his class graduated next week, he would be announced as the winner of a two-year traveling fellowship to France. There he would study with Gustav Scholl himself, who now had a studio in Paris. Fairview High and Greenbaum seemed far away.

"You've changed, you know," Harber said suddenly. "My only doubt about giving you that scholarship in 1948 was a personal one. When you came to interview with me, you were cocky—too sure of yourself. Now you're still sure of yourself, as you ought to be. But you've learned to take criticism, and to know what your limitations are."

Mark grinned. "Come to think of it," he said, "I suppose I was pretty unbearable during that interview. This teacher I just mentioned to you—Greenbaum—may have been partly responsible. I got so little praise from him that I felt I had to blow my own horn."

"Greenbaum?" asked Dean Harber, raising his eyebrows. "Greenbaum never praised you?"

"Why, no," Mark answered. "As I say, he always had it in for me."

Harber rose from his desk, and walked over to a filing cabinet. After leafing through several folders, he finally pulled out a piece of paper. "Read this," he suggested, handing it to Mark.

Mark took the paper, unfolded it carefully, and read.

Fairview High School
Fairview, Ohio
Department of Art
June 30, 1948

Dear Dean Harber:

I presume upon your time to write this letter about Mark Spencer, a candidate for the Bryant Art School four-year scholarship, because I feel that the answers to questions on the standard blank do not fully suggest this boy's unusual qualifications.

You have already had one interview with Mark Spencer. I daresay that you found him vain of his talents, overconfident of his prospects. I have found him so, too, and have done what I could to discourage these traits.

I hope I am not out of order if I suggest that this impression is a misleading one. Mark Spencer's faults, such as they are, are the faults of a boy whose talent is truly extraordinary. He is still young; he will grow up; and I am confident that he will become a distinguished artist. If he is too ready to acknowledge his own ability, it is only because that ability is great, and is so much the center of his life and ambitions. He is compelled, more than the ordinary person, to believe in himself.

Throughout his high school years, Mark Spencer has never been sure that he would be able to continue his study of art. There is little money in his family, and his chance to succeed at what he wants most to do depends entirely upon the recognition he can win from such "powers" as you represent. Once he is assured that his chance will be given him, he will be less insecure, more able to take criticism and to be what he has it in him to be.

I do not urge that your scholarship be awarded to Mark Spencer for personal reasons; his talent it too pronounced to make that necessary. But I do urge that his candidacy should not, for personal reasons, be viewed with disfavor.

Very truly yours,
Thomas J. Greenbaum

"It was this letter," Dean Harber observed as Mark finished reading, "that helped to clear away my last doubts as to the advisability of awarding you the Bryant scholarship. I was convinced that your Mr. Greenbaum knew the boy he spoke of. And," Harber added smiling, "I wasn't wrong."

Mark, staring at the letter, didn't reply. "June 30, 1948," the date on the letterhead—that would have been four, possibly five, days after the June afternoon on which he had given Old

Greenbaum a piece of his mind. Then Greenbaum had written this letter. Mark wondered unhappily whether he himself could ever write such a letter after such an incident.

His eye caught one of Greenbaum's phrases and fixed on it—"to be what he has it in him to be." That was how it was, then. More than Scholl, more than even Mark himself, Old Greenbaum must have had a high vision of what Mark had it in him to be; a vision so determined that he was willing to sacrifice his student's affection for himself as a teacher in order to further his future as an artist.

"You say that Greenbaum 'had it in' for you," Harber observed. "I can see from your expression that this letter has suggested otherwise. Why don't you let me give you an extra ticket for the commencement exercises?" he suggested. "I have an idea that Mr. Thomas Greenbaum would be the proudest man in the auditorium if he could see you walk across that platform as the winner of the two-year fellowship to Paris."

Mark looked up, his face red, as he put the letter back on Harber's desk. Harber was right—he knew that now. No one he had known in his life would be so proud of his present success as Old Greenbaum. No one he had known deserved so well to be proud.

Mark's glance fell again on the old watercolor which Harber had pulled out of his folder. He would never again, he reflected, look at this watercolor without a stab of regret. The quality of design which he had sensed at the beginning of this interview had taken on a dreadful symmetry.

Vividly, remembered images from the past flooded before him. Greenbaum's knobby finger on his work: "Erase those lines—do it again—you can do in one line what you've done in several." Greenbaum's cool, appraising eyes taking in a finished sketch:

"Not bad—and not so good as you think it is, either." And then the image which came not from memory but from imagination; an old man sitting down to write a letter full of understanding and faith.

"Shall we send him a ticket?" the dean was saying.

Mark shook his head. For no ticket could now be sent—no grateful gesture was any longer possible.

"Thank you, Dean Harber," he said. "I wish I could. But Mr. Greenbaum died two years ago."

Mary Dirlam

Mary Dirlam wrote for periodicals during the early to middle years of the twentieth century.

A LITTLE
BROWN BULB

Leeta McCully Cherry

*A very foolish thing to do!" declared the older teacher.
Much better to have grown the bulbs in the classroom.
Little did she know.*

*A*nd so," Miss Kendall went on in her sweet voice, "all the flowers and grasses sleep in the warm brown earth until the sunlight creeps down to waken them in the springtime, and Old Mother Nature whispers softly, 'Come, little children, it is time to waken now!' Then way down in the earth the little bulbs and roots begin to stir; up, up, up they come until their little green heads peep up at sunny skies and the warm winds kiss them as they hurry past. And all the while, down in their little brown houses beneath the ground, each little plant is preparing its lovely coloring and its fragrance, until presently it sends them forth in a little bud which swells and swells until before very long a wonderful flower blooms among the green leaves. Isn't it wonderful, children?" She paused and held up a little round brown bulb.

"Just see this plain, ugly-looking little thing! Who could ever imagine that it holds within it all the fragrance and beauty of what may be a rosy hyacinth, a blue one, or a sunny golden yellow one? Yet all this loveliness is there, hidden safely away, just waiting for a little care and attention to make it bloom for us in all its beauty. And now, to each little girl and boy I am going to give one of these little brown bulbs to take home. I want you to plant it carefully in a little pot, keep it in the dark for six weeks before you bring it to the sunshine, and then when it has grown into a lovely flower we are going to bring all of them back to school and use them for decoration when we have our spring concert for which we are practicing."

The class of shabby little kindergartners relaxed with a long sigh of joy. To have a lovely flower of their very own! Why, it seemed almost too good to be true. For those little children lived deep in the heart of a great city where all the flowers they knew grew in the windows of the florists' shops or else in flower beds in the parks, where little children must not ever touch them. And now Teacher said they could take one of these queer little bulbs home, and by and by there would be a beautiful flower to bring back to school. It did seem strange how a flower like those of the florists' shops could come from those ugly brown things, but of course if teacher said so, it must be true.

Little Rosa Blondini's dark eyes shone like stars as she rushed into her tumble-down little home that noon with the precious bulb held close in her brown little fist. Shouting to make herself heard over the baby's fretful cries, she called, "Ma! Look what Teacher gave me. It's a flower!"

Her mother raised tired eyes from the stove and glanced at the little brown bulb in Rosa's hand. "Huh!" she grunted. "It's an onion you got—that's all!"

An onion! Rosa's face fell. But no! That couldn't be. Teacher said it was a flower—a flower it must be! "No," she cried. "You plant it in some earth, and soon it grows a flower."

"There's no earth around here this time of year," her mother told her.

Big tears came into the dark eyes. Of course there wasn't.

"Aw, cheer up." Tony spoke from his corner. "I'll get you some dirt if that's all you want for your onion."

"Get it now?" Rosa questioned swiftly. "Teacher said right away to plant it. And 'tisn't an onion. It's a lovely flower sometime."

Tony grinned. "All right! Mebbe you're right—we'll see! Come on down to the cellar and we'll dig some dirt."

Happily Rosa trotted after him, and together they found an old tomato can in which to plant the little brown bulb. "Now, what you goin' to do with it—eh?" asked Tony. "The baby'll dig it up most likely when you go to school."

"In the dark it stays, Teacher says, for six weeks, with water every day," Rosa explained patiently.

"Better leave it in the cellar, then," advised Tony. "But you'll forget to water it like as not."

Rosa didn't forget. Every day, despite her fears of the dark cellar, she carried water down to the little pot. Teacher had said there was a little flower there, and Teacher had never failed her yet!

"Ain't you scared of mice and things down there?" Tony teased her.

"W-e-ll," Rosa answered, "I gotta water my flower anyway. Often Teacher asks about it, and she says there's nothing in the dark to hurt me, either."

"It's a good job you got something to make you believe that then," said her mother not quite so crossly as usual.

One day the miracle happened. Two stout little shoots of green glimmered in the darkness as Rosa bent over the pot. "Oh, Ma!" she shrilled up the stairs. "My flower's come! Come down and see it, Ma. Oh, you oughta see it, Ma! Come quick!"

Something in the child's voice touched the tired woman vaguely, and rather to her own surprise Mrs. Blondini found herself going down to see what Rosa had. Together they bent over the pot.

"Sure," said the mother, poking it with her finger, "it's going to be a flower, maybe. It should have some light now. Put it over by the cellar window."

Together they cleared away the rubbish and placed the sturdy little green shoots where the light could fall on them.

Each day Rosa raced home from school, and each day the little plant greeted her more sturdily. At school the children talked incessantly of their plants, and as Rosa's had been the first to show above the earth, her joy knew no bounds. "Teacher says to put my flower in the sunshine now—in the window," she announced one day on her return.

So up from the cellar it came and found a place on the window ledge facing the street. How Tony laughed when he saw it. "Why," he said, "I'll be eating that for green onions some night for my supper!"

"You're to leave Rosa's plant alone, now—all of you!" It was Father Blondini's voice from the stove, and at the unusual tone Mother Blondini looked at him wistfully. To her surprise he grinned at her amiably and took the crowing baby from her arms.

It was really surprising how that plant grew—how strong and richly green it became in the warm sunshine. And then one wonderful day Mother Blondini saw a bud swelling out among the green leaves. *How Rosa will like that!* she thought, raising her dark eyes to see if the child was coming down the street. Then she saw something else. The window was dirty! Terribly dirty! Strange she hadn't noticed it before. *I must wash that window,* she thought with new determination, and straightway set to work.

Rosa was jubilant over the tight little spear of close-sheathed buds. Tony must see it, Father Blondini must see it, even the baby was lifted up to look. "And how nice the window looks, Mother! Just like no glass at all, and the sun shines through like diamonds. How good you were to wash it." And she threw her arms about her mother's neck and kissed her. Sudden tears rose in Mother's eyes; caresses had become scarce indeed in the Blondini household of late years. She glanced about the littered and dirty room with new vision, as she moved about setting the dinner in place.

When all was quiet afterward and baby asleep in his crib, Mrs. Blondini attacked that room in real earnest. Down came the

dingy curtains, and to such good purpose did she work that when
Father came in at night he stopped in the doorway from sheer
astonishment. Clean white curtains were looped back at the
window, the big black stove radiated cheer and cleanliness, and
the delicious aroma of a well-cooked stew filled the room.
Mother's sleek black hair lay round her head in smooth, well-
brushed coils; gone were the mussy boudoir cap and the soiled
old wrapper. Mother Blondini was straight and slender in a clean
house dress and apron, and her eyes shone with a new light as
they rested on Father.

"Ain't it grand, Father?" called Rosa, quite unmindful of
troublesome grammar. "It's just like school now—it's so nice!"

"Well, Wife," grinned Father, giving Mother a pat as he
passed, "I don't know whether this is where I live or not. You
look so grand I hardly know you! I guess I'll have to scrub myself
up clean now or I'll not get any supper, eh?"

Mother laughed like a girl as he passed.

All the time the little plant kept on growing and the close
green bud grew fatter and fatter. "You ought to cover up that old
tomato can with something," Tony said one day. "I'll get you a
piece of green paper to put around it like they do in the flower
windows." That evening he and Rosa spent ever so long fluting
and pinning the green crepe paper until it stood out proudly
about the little plant.

Then one day the buds had swelled enough to show the color
peeping through. "It's going to be rose!" announced Father after
close inspection. "Just like your name, Rosa," smiled Mother.

It was hard to be patient now, but at last one morning when
Rosa got up Mother pointed silently to the window, and there it
stood in all its beauty, surely the most wonderful hyacinth anyone
had ever seen! Its great flower spike was a glowing rose among

the green, and each little close-growing flower was as perfect as a tiny lily bell. And the fragrance! The whole room was full of it. Rosa thought her joy was complete, and even Tony was speechless before such loveliness as he had never seen before.

For weeks the kindergarten had been practicing for their spring concert, and now that the flowers were blooming, Teacher announced the great event for next Friday.

"I do so hope the mothers will come out this time," she said to the primary teacher at lunch hour that day. "They never seem to take a bit of interest in what the children do at school. That's why I gave them the hyacinths to grow at home."

"Which was a very foolish thing to do, I'm afraid, my dear!" said the older teacher skeptically. "If you had grown the bulbs here at school the children could have watched them just as well, and you would have been sure of your flowers. You'll be lucky if there are ten bulbs brought back."

"O Miss Norton," cried the younger teacher, "you've no idea how interested the children have been! Why, little Rosa Blondini—"

"My dear girl, you'll never succeed in rousing the Blondini family to take interest in anything; so don't set your young heart on getting your plant from them."

"Well, say, have you walked past their house lately? You wouldn't know it! Do go home that way tonight, just to please me. And be sure to come in to the concert tomorrow afternoon—you'll be surprised!" called Evelyn Kendall as the older teacher went back to her room.

The concert was almost over when the primary teacher opened the door and slipped in. All the front of the room was abloom with pots of fragrant hyacinths in all stages of development and all sorts of pots. It seemed as if all the mothers of the neighborhood were there, listening in rapt attention to the gay little songs and choruses of the kindergarten, and right in the front row sat Mrs. Blondini, neat and pretty, with the baby on her lap. In the very center of all, on a table quite by itself, stood the glorious rose hyacinth that was Rosa Blondini's, and it was plainly marked so that all could see, "First Prize." As the concert closed each child presented her own hyacinth to her mother, a little gift of love, but not a face there shone with such honest pride as did those of Rosa Blondini and her smiling mother.

"My dear girl," warmly congratulated the once doubting primary teacher later on, "how ever did you get all those mothers so interested? You have scored a veritable triumph. Even Mrs. Blondini!"

"Why, I didn't do it at all!" laughed Miss Kendall happily. "It was all the work of those little brown bulbs!"

Leeta McCully Cherry

Leeta McCully Cherry wrote for inspirational magazines during the first half of the twentieth century.

MOUNTAINS
TO CLIMB

Russell Gordon Carter

artin Bligh knew he'd picked a tough job, but he didn't then know just how tough. The fourteen boys were determined not to learn—and to get his goat.

They succeeded at both.

*M*r. Rayburn, the state superintendent of education, glanced up from the papers on his desk and carefully removed his glasses. His eyes were troubled as he turned toward the tall blond young man seated beside him.

"I am sorry you are not older and more experienced," he said. "Do you realize that if I send you to Pine River, you will be teaching boys who are only a few years younger than yourself?"

Martin Bligh nodded.

"And you realize also, do you not, that those boys proved altogether too big a problem for their previous teacher, whose place I now have to fill?"

"Yes, sir, I know that."

Mr. Rayburn hesitated. Not merely the applicant's youth and inexperience troubled him, but something in his manner the superintendent found far from reassuring, an apparent casualness that he was not quite able to understand.

"I should like to know," the superintendent said abruptly, "why, in your application for a teaching job, you expressed a preference for a place in the Pine River country."

Martin smiled rather self-consciously. "To be quite frank, it was because of the mountains," he replied.

"I'm afraid I don't understand you." Mr. Rayburn lifted his eyebrows.

"Well, I've always been fond of mountains," Martin added, "and of course if I were located in the Pine River country, I'd be able to do some climbing."

"Oh," said the superintendent. Leaning back in his chair, he fixed his gaze on the ceiling. He suddenly wanted to laugh, mirthlessly, cynically. Never in his life had he met so unpromising an applicant!

"Of course," said Martin, "I think I can teach the boys something. If I didn't, I'd tell you so, frankly."

Mr. Rayburn rose and began to pace the room. He asked himself what he should do. The school at Pine River was without a teacher, it was scheduled to begin at once, and the young man seated beside the desk was the only available candidate for the place. Would it be worth while to give him a chance? Or would it be better to postpone the opening of the school until a better teacher could be found?

At last the superintendent came to a decision. Pausing beside the desk, he said abruptly, "Very well, we'll see what you can do! I want to open the school on time or it would have a bad effect on the boys. The boys would be puffed up to think they had driven their teacher out, and no one to replace him. So good luck to you, and I hope you may succeed!"

"I intend to succeed!" Martin replied. For the first time Mr. Rayburn observed determination as well as good humor in the set of the young man's mouth.

Late that afternoon Martin was on the train speeding northward.

The school at Pine River was a small square building of gray shingles on the northern outskirts of the village. Seated at his desk on the slightly raised platform, Martin was again aware of mountains: they loomed cold and blue through the windows above the heads of the fourteen boys who had assembled, reluctantly, after a long vacation. He said to himself, *This afternoon I'll do some climbing!* Glancing again toward his pupils, he said:

"Now, fellows, we're all going to be together here in the class-room; so let's get acquainted. My name is Mr. Bligh and—"

At that point one of the boys at the back of the room uttered a kind of snort that was clearly intended to provoke disorder.

"We seem to have a pig in the room," observed Martin; then he added, "Now I'm going to ask each fellow to tell me his name. When I come to the pig, he can snort if he wants to. Let's begin on the right—"

"Joseph Howard," said a thick-set, red-haired boy in the front seat.

"We call him Red!" a boy in the other aisle added.

Again laughter came and Martin smiled. "Who's the boy behind Red Howard?" he asked.

"William Gibson."

"And the fellows can call you Bill, is that right?"

"Yes."

"Next," said Martin. "First give me your real name, then your nickname. That'll save time."

"Duncan Hall—Dunc for short."

"Next," said Martin.

During the quarter of an hour that followed numerous attempts were made at horseplay, but Martin's good humor was disarming. He had a good memory, and when all fourteen of the boys had given their names he was able to repeat them without a mistake. That impressed the class, and he felt that he had made a good beginning.

His hopes received a jolt, however, when he began the serious work of the day. The boys were not interested in study.

At the end of the day Martin felt worn out. He climbed no mountains that afternoon; instead he went to his room and sat for a long time pondering; wondering how he might do better.

The next day was a repetition of the first. If the teacher entered into the spirit of the boys' foibles, they were satisfied; that they found him likeable was apparent. As soon as he took up the serious work of the class, they returned to their old attitude of indifference.

A week passed with no signs of improvement. During that week Martin viewed the mountains only from a distance. His hiking shoes were under the bed, where he had placed them the first day. He recalled his confident remark to the superintendent: "I intend to succeed!" He had not succeeded and his pride was touched. He resolved to do no climbing until he had gained the mastery over his class, until he was a teacher in fact as well as in name!

Thus far he had managed to maintain his good humor and to conceal his discouragement, but one day an event occurred that proved to be a little too much for him. For the past two or three mornings a few of the boys had been arriving five or ten minutes late. On this particular morning six of them were absent when class began. He inquired if anyone knew where they were and received no response, although he guessed from their attitude of suppressed mystery that those present knew something concerning the absent ones.

"Well, let's begin," he said and proceeded with the assignment in arithmetic.

Three quarters of an hour later, while he was in the midst of an explanation, the six boys entered the classroom and, with an appearance of indifference, took their seats. The rest of the class began to titter, but this ceased abruptly as Martin strode from the blackboard to the desk.

"Fellows," he said sharply, "you're playing a dirty game! You're not playing the game fair! If this were football and I were your coach, you six fellows who just came in would be off the team for the rest of the season!" He pointed his finger at Douglas Crandall, one of the late arrivals. "Crandall," he said, "stand up!"

The boy hesitated, but something in Martin's eyes made him obey; he slouched reluctantly to his feet.

"Now, Crandall, what have you got to say? Why did the six of you decide to come in three quarters of an hour late?"

Douglas Crandall shrugged his shoulders and made no reply. Again there was tittering, and Crandall looked pleased and important.

Martin's hands were cold and trembling. He knew it was a mistake to allow the class to see that he was angry, but he could not help it. "Sit down!" he ordered. And then in a quivering voice he added, "If a thing like this happens again, there's going to be trouble!"

Despite the force of his utterance, he knew that he had made a poor impression. The boys had "got a rise" out of him and were delighted.

While the class was writing, he sat with gaze fixed beyond the windows. There, far off, were the mountains that he longed to climb. He remembered his resolve to do no climbing until he had gained the mastery over his class. Disheartened by the recent encounter, he wondered if he had not been rather foolish to make such a resolution. Why not let the class go its own way?

A cloud passed across the sun, and the mountains were almost black. Martin Bligh had not seen them before in that somber mood, and he was impressed by their beauty and strength. They seemed somehow to stir him to unknown depths; something was heartening and inspiring in their massive strength and steadfastness. *No,* he decided, *if I can't handle these boys, I don't deserve the fun of climbing!*

The morning passed without incident, and Martin felt that possibly his sharp words and display of anger might have had a good effect after all; but at the afternoon session, to his surprise and dismay only one boy, Duncan Hall, was in his seat at the appointed hour! Martin waited ten minutes, and still none of the others appeared.

As the minutes passed, he felt a growing conviction: he had told the class that in the event of further tardiness trouble would result, and now they had deliberately accepted his challenge!

"What's become of the others?" he inquired abruptly.

Duncan Hall lowered his gaze.

Martin walked down the aisle and seated himself on the desk next to Duncan's. "Look here, Dunc," he said, smiling, "I don't want you to squeal—of course not! But I think I know as well as you do what's happened; the rest of the class intend to find out if I meant what I said this morning."

The boy lifted his head. "How did you know that?" he asked in surprise.

Martin shrugged his shoulders. "Why didn't you join them?" he inquired.

The boy moistened his lips. "Because—well, because I didn't think it was the square thing to do!"

"I'm grateful to you, Duncan!"

Something in Martin's voice touched the boy. Lifting his eyes abruptly, he said, "Mr. Bligh, I don't care whether they call me a squealer or not! It's true, what you said, and the whole bunch of them are in Red Howard's cabin down the path. They intend to stay there until school's almost out and then come in, just to see what you'll do!"

Martin walked with slow steps to the window. Again, for a brief moment, he felt the temptation to let the class go its own way; but in front of him were the mountains, strong, steadfast, somehow inspiring! He turned and strode to the desk. Picking up his geography book, he said to Duncan Hall, "Come along!"

A few moments later he and Duncan were outside, following the path that led downhill through the woods. At the end of perhaps ten minutes they came to a small rough shack beside a stream, and there were the rest of the class, some of them inside the shack, some lounging about on the grass outside. They greeted the teacher with looks of startled surprise.

Martin glanced at his watch. "All right, fellows," he said as if everything were natural and orderly, "everybody inside the cabin. We're almost twenty minutes late, but we'll make up for it."

The boys obeyed him wonderingly, crowding into the shack.

"Now, fellows," he added, "since you seem to like this place better than the schoolhouse, we'll hold class right here." He paused impressively. "Ever since I came to Pine River you fellows have been trying to get my goat. Well, you got it this morning, but I'll promise you you'll never get it again! I was sent up here to teach you something, and believe me, I'm going to do it!

"Of course," Martin continued, "if I wanted to, I could go to your parents and tell them you went off in the woods when you ought to have been at school. In that case some of you would get a licking. But I don't want that to happen, and I don't believe you do! Now for the geography lesson! Red Howard, since you own this cabin, you'll have the honor of answering the first question: What is an isthmus? First, give the definition, and then take that stick and draw one for me on the blackboard!"

The boy looked bewildered. "On the blackboard?" he repeated.

"Yes," said Martin and pointed to the dirt floor.

The others grinned as Red Howard stepped forward.

That was the beginning of Martin's triumph. Despite the cramped quarters, he kept the class in the cabin for the full period. At the end of it he asked the boys where they would prefer to meet thereafter, in the crowded cabin again or in the schoolroom where all might be comfortable. They voted in rather a shame-faced matter for the schoolroom.

The next morning they were all on time. During the days that followed it was apparent that their attitude had changed for the better. Less horseplay was seen and some of the boys began to show an interest in the work.

Meanwhile, thrilled by his triumph, Martin devoted much of his spare time to devising new means of holding their interest. He climbed no mountains; but when the term finally ended, he had the satisfaction of knowing that he had really taught the boys something.

The day that followed the end of the term he was obliged to return to the city, without having climbed a single one of the peaks that surrounded Pine River Village. The day after that he again confronted the state superintendent in his office.

"I have had some exceedingly good reports of your work!" Mr. Rayburn exclaimed as he clasped Martin's hand. "I needn't tell you I am delighted, for I admit I had grave misgivings."

"Yes, I know that, Mr. Rayburn."

"How about next semester?" the superintendent interrupted him. "Would you care to take the school again?"

"Yes, I would, because this semester I feel that I've done nothing more than just make a start."

"Good!" said Mr. Rayburn. He added casually, "You were interested, I believe, in the mountains up there. Did you climb any?"

Martin suddenly laughed. "Why, yes," he replied whimsically.

"I climbed fourteen of them, but the curious thing about it, Mr. Rayburn, is that there's not a speck of mud or dirt on my hiking shoes!"

For an instant the superintendent looked puzzled; then his eyes crinkled in an understanding smile.

Russell Gordon Carter
(1892–1957)

Russell Gordon Carter was born in Trenton, N.J. Besides the hundreds of stories he wrote for magazines during the first half of the twentieth century, he also wrote the four-volume Bob Hanson series (1921–23), the twelve-volume Patriot Lad series (1923–36), *Teen-Age Historical Stories* (1948), *Teen-Age Animal Stories* (1949), and *Mr. Whatley Enjoys Himself* (1954).

THE TALLEST
ANGEL

Author Unknown

Miss Ellis was sorry for the sad-faced hunchback girl, but being sorry changed almost nothing. It certainly didn't make Dory feel loved or a part of the class.

So what could she do?

God doesn't love me!" The words echoed sharply through the thoughts of Miss Ellis as she looked around the fourth-grade schoolroom. Her gaze skipped lightly over the many bent heads and then rested on one in particular. "God doesn't love me!" The words had struck Miss Ellis's heart so painfully that her mouth opened slightly in mute protest.

The child under Miss Ellis's troubled study lifted her head for a moment, scanned her classmates briefly, then bent to her book again.

Ever since the first day of school, Miss Ellis had been hurt and troubled by those bitter assertions. "God doesn't love me!" The words had come from the small nine-year-old girl who stirred again restively under the continued scrutiny of Miss Ellis. Then, bending her head to her own desk, Miss Ellis prayed in her heart for the nth time: *Help her, dear God, and help me to help her. Please show Dory that You do love her, too.*

Dory sat with her geography book open upon her desk, but the thoughts that raced through her mind were not concerned with the capital of Ohio. A moment before she had felt the warm eyes of Miss Ellis upon her, and now angry sentences played tag with each other in her bowed head. Once again she heard the calm voice of Miss Ellis.

"God wants us to be happy in His love"—Dory laughed bitterly to herself. How could anyone be happy with a hunched back and leg braces!

"God loves everyone," Miss Ellis had said, to which Dory had angrily replied, "But He doesn't love me—that's why He made me ugly and crippled."

"God is good."

"God is not good to me. He's mean to me! That's what—to let me grow so crooked."

Dory raised her head and looked at the children around her. Mary Ann had long golden curls; Dory had straight brown hair, pulled back tight and braided into an unlovely pigtail. Jeanetta had china blue eyes that twinkled like evening stars; Dory had brown eyes that seemed smoky, so full of bitterness were they. Ellen Sue had a pink rosebud mouth that readily spread into a happy smile. Well, Ellen Sue could smile. She had a lovely dimpled face and ruffled, ribboned dresses. But why should Dory smile? Her mouth was straight and tight, and her body was hunched and twisted. Anyone would laugh to see ruffles on *her* dresses. No pink and blue dresses for her, only straight dark gowns that hung like sacks over her small hunched frame.

Suddenly hate and anger so filled the heart of the little girl that she felt she must get away from this roomful of straight-bodied children or choke. She signaled her desire to Miss Ellis, who nodded permission.

There was neither pity nor laughter in the eyes that followed Dory to the door, only casual indifference. The children had long since accepted Dory as she was. No one ever jeered at her awkwardness, nor did anyone fuss over her in pity. The children did not mean to be unkind, but knowing the limits of Dory's mobility, they usually ran off to their active games, leaving her a lonely little spectator.

Miss Ellis saw the children settle back to their studies as the door closed after Dory. She stared at the door, not seeing the door at all, only the small, hunchbacked girl.

What can I do to help her to be happy? she pondered. *What can anyone say or do to comfort and encourage such a child?*

She had talked to Dory's parents and had found them to be of little help. They seemed inclined to feel that Dory's crippled condition was a blot upon *them,* one that they did not deserve.

Miss Ellis had urged them not to try to explain Dory's condition but to accept it and try to seek God's blessings through it. They were almost scornful of the idea that any blessing could be found in a crippled, unhappy child, but they did agree to come to church and to bring Dory as often as possible.

Please help Dory, prayed Miss Ellis. *Help Dory and her parents, too.* Then the hall bell sounded, and Miss Ellis arose to dismiss her class.

❧

The reds, yellows and greens of autumn faded into the white of winter. The Christmas season was unfolding in the room. Tiny Christmas trees stood shyly on the windowsills. A great green wreath covered the door. Its silver bells jingled whenever the door moved, and the delighted giggles of the children echoed in return. The blue-white shadows of a winter afternoon were creeping across the snow as Miss Ellis watched the excited children set up the manger scene on the low sand table.

Christmas, thought Miss Ellis, *is a time of peace and joy. Even the children feel the spirit and try to be nicer to one another.*

"Is your Christmas dress done yet, Ellen Sue?"

Without waiting for an answer, Mary Ann chattered on, "Mother got material for mine today—it's red, real red velvet. Oh, I can hardly wait, can you?"

"Mine is all done but the hem." Ellen Sue fairly trembled with excitement. "It's pink, with rosebuds made of ribbon."

Miss Ellis smiled, remembering the thrill of the Christmas dresses of her own girlhood. How carefully they were planned, and how lovingly her mother had made each one. Miss Ellis leaned back to cherish the memories a moment longer. Then a movement caught her eye. Slowly, furtively, with storm-filled eyes, Dory was backing away from the chattering children. Miss Ellis's heart stirred with sympathy as she watched the unhappy child ease herself into her chair, pull a book from her desk, and bend her head over it. *She isn't studying,* thought Miss Ellis. *She is only pretending—to cover up her misery.*

Dory stared at the book in front of her, fighting against the tears that demanded release. What if one of the girls had asked her about *her* Christmas dress? Her Christmas dress indeed! Would anyone call a brown sack of a dress a Christmas dress? Would the children laugh? No, Dory knew the girls wouldn't laugh. They would just feel sorry for her and her shapeless dress. Sometimes that was almost worse than if they would laugh. At least then she would have an excuse to pour out the angry words that crowded into her throat.

"Dory." A warm voice broke in upon her thoughts. "Dory, will you help me with these Christmas decorations? You could walk along and hold them for me while I pin them up, please."

Dory arose, thankful for the diversion and thankful to be near Miss Ellis. The silver tinsel was pleasant to hold, and Miss Ellis always made her feel so much better.

Slowly they proceeded around the room, draping the tinsel garland as they went. The babble of voices in the corner by the sand table took on a new note, an insistent clamoring tone that finally burst forth in a rush of small bodies in the direction of Miss Ellis.

"Please, Miss Ellis, can I be Mary in the Christmas program?"

"Miss Ellis, I'd like to be Joseph."

"I should be Mary because I can't sing in the angel choir."

Miss Ellis raised her hand for quiet. After a moment she began:

"I've already chosen the ones who will play the parts of Mary, Joseph, the shepherds, and the angel choir."

"Tell us the names; tell us the names now," the children chorused.

"All right," agreed Miss Ellis as she reached for a sheet of paper from her desk. "Here they are: Sue Ellen will be Mary; Daniel will be Joseph; John, Allen and Morris will be the shepherds. All the rest of you will be choir angels—"

Miss Ellis scanned the eager hopeful faces around her till she saw the upturned face of Dory. There was no eager hope in her small pinched face. Dory felt from bitter experience that no one wanted a hunchback in a program. Miss Ellis could not bear the numb resignation on that small white face. Almost without realizing what she was saying, she finished the sentence. "All will be choir angels except Dory." There was a moment of hushed surprise. "Dory will be the special angel who talks to the shepherds."

All the children gasped and turned to look at Dory. Dory, a special angel? They had never thought of that. As realization penetrated Dory's amazement, a slow smile relaxed the pinched features, a little candle flame of happiness shone in the brown eyes.

Her eyes are lovely when she's happy, marveled Miss Ellis. *Oh, help her to be happy more often!*

The hall bell sounded the end of another school day, and soon all the children had bidden Miss Ellis good-by as they hurried from the room.

All but one. All but Dory. She stood very still, as if clinging to a magic moment for as long as possible. The lights had flickered out of her eyes, and her face seemed whiter than ever before.

Miss Ellis knelt and took Dory's cold little hands in her own. "What is it, Dory? Don't you want to be a special angel, after all?"

"I do, I do—" Dory's voice broke. "But—but—I'll be a horrid hunchbacked angel. Everyone will stare at me and laugh because angels are straight and beauti—" Dory's small body shook with uncontrollable sobs.

"Listen to me, Dory," Miss Ellis began slowly. "You are going to be my special angel. Somehow I'm going to make you look straight and beautiful, like real angels. Will you just be happy, Dory, and let me plan it all out? Then I'll tell you all about it."

Dory lifted her head hopefully. "Do you think you can, Miss Ellis, do you think you can?"

"I know I can, Dory. Smile now; you're so pretty when you smile. And say over and over, 'God loves me, God loves me.' That will make you want to smile. Will you try it, Dory?"

A shadow of disbelief crossed Dory's face. Then she brightened with resolution.

"I'll say it, Miss Ellis, and if you can make me look like a straight angel, I'll try to believe it."

"That's the spirit, Dory. Good-by, now, and have nice dreams tonight."

Dory went to the door, paused a moment, then turned again to Miss Ellis.

"Yes, Dory, is there something else?"

Dory hesitated for a long moment. Then she said slowly: "Do you think I could look like a tall angel, too? I'm smaller than anyone else because my back is so bent. Do you think I could look like a tall angel?"

"I'm sure we can make you look tall," promised Miss Ellis recklessly.

Dory sighed with satisfaction and let the door swing shut behind her. The silver bells on the Christmas wreath jingled merrily, almost mockingly.

What have I done? thought Miss Ellis soberly. *I have promised a little crooked girl that she will be a tall, straight angel. I haven't the slightest idea how I am going to do it. Dear God, please help me—show me the way. For the first time since I've known her, I have seen Dory happy. Please help her to be happy in Your love, dear God. Show me the way to help her.*

Miss Ellis went to sleep that night with the prayer still in her heart.

Morning came crisp and clear. Lacy frills of frost hung daintily from every branch and bush. Miss Ellis rubbed her eyes and looked out of her window. The sparkling white beauty of the morning reminded her of angels. Angels! She recalled her promise. She had dreamed of angels, too. What was the dream about, what was it?

Miss Ellis tapped her finger against her lip in concentration. Suddenly, as if a dark door had opened to the sunshine, the dream, the whole angel plan, swept into her mind. Idea after idea tumbled about like dancing sunbeams. She must hurry and dress; she must get to the schoolhouse early to talk to Joe, the janitor. Joe could do anything, and she was sure that Joe would help her.

At the door of the school she scarcely paused to stomp the snow from her boots. Quickly she went down to the furnace room where Joe was stoking coal into the hungry furnace.

"Joe," she began, "I need your help. I've got a big job ahead of me. I'm going to make little Dory Saunders into a tall, straight angel for our Christmas pageant."

Joe thumped his shovel down, looked at her intently, and

scratched his head. "You certainly did pick yourself a job, Miss Ellis. How you going to do all this, and where do I figure?"

"It's like this, Joe." She outlined her plan to him, and Joe agreed to it.

Miss Ellis went lightly up the steps to her fourth grade room. She greeted the children cheerily, smiling warmly at Dory. Dory returned the smile, with the candle flames of happiness glowing again in her eyes.

For Dory the day was enchanted. Round-faced angels smiled at her through the Os in her arithmetic book. The time passed dreamily on whirring angel wings. At last school was over, and she was alone with Miss Ellis, waiting to hear the marvelous plan that would make her a straight and beautiful angel.

"I've thought it all out, Dory." Miss Ellis pulled Dory close as she explained the plan. "Mrs. Brown and I are going to make you a long white gown and wings, and Joe will fix you up so you will be the tallest angel of all. But Dory, let's keep it a secret until the night of the program, shall we?"

Dory nodded vigorously. She couldn't speak. The vision was too lovely for words; so she just nodded and hugged Miss Ellis as tight as her thin arms could squeeze. Then she limped from the room.

Dory had never felt such happiness. Now she really had a place in the scheme of events. At least until Christmas, she felt, she really belonged with the other children. She was really like other children. Maybe God loved even her.

At last the night of the program came. Carols of praise to the newborn King rang through the school.

Now it was time for the Christmas pageant. Soft music invited a quiet mood, and the audience waited for the curtains to open upon a shepherd scene.

The sky was dark as the shepherds sat huddled around their fire. Then suddenly a bright light burst over the scene. The audience gasped in surprise. High up on a pedestal, dressed in a gown of shimmering white satin, Dory raised her arms in salutation.

"Fear not." Her face was radiant as she spoke. "For, behold, I bring you good tidings of great joy, which shall be to all people." Her voice gathered conviction as she continued, "For unto you is born this day in the city of David a Saviour, which is Christ, the Lord."

The triumphant ring in her voice carried to the choir, and the children sang, "Glory to God in the highest, and on earth peace, good will toward men," as they had never sung before.

Dory's father blinked hard at the tears that stung his eyes, and he thought in his heart, *Why, she's a beautiful child. Why doesn't Martha curl her hair and put a ribbon in it?*

Dory's mother closed her eyes on the lovely vision, praying silently, *Forgive me, God; I haven't appreciated the good things about Dory because I've been so busy complaining about her misfortunes.*

The sound of the carols sung by the choir died away, and the curtains silently closed.

Miss Ellis hurried backstage and lifted Dory from her high pedestal.

"Dory," she asked softly, "what happened? How did you feel when you were the angel? Something wonderful happened to you. I saw it in your face."

Dory hesitated, "You'll laugh—"

"Never, never, Dory, I promise!"

"Well, while I was saying the angel message, I began to feel taller and taller and real straight." She paused and looked intently at Miss Ellis.

"Go on, dear," urged Miss Ellis gently. "What else?"

"Well, I didn't feel my braces any more. And do you know what?"

"No, what? Tell me."

"Right then I knew it was true. God *does* love me."

"Dory, as long as you know that is true, you'll never be really unhappy again. And someday, my dear, you will stand straight and tall and beautiful among the real angels in heaven."

UNLOVED,
UNWANTED, UNTIL . . .

Lola Hovener

A truant officer brought the belligerent twelve-year-old to her new teacher, Mr. Kelly. She hated him instantly, just as she hated the whole world. No one in the whole world loved her, cared for her, was willing to be a friend to her.

Then Mr. Kelly offered her a glass of milk.

*M*y first meeting with Mr. Kelly was two days after the new term began. He was my seventh-grade teacher, tall, thin and red-headed. I was brought to him by a truant officer.

"You've got a real corker here, Kelly," he said. "Let me know if she gives you any trouble."

I slunk off to the back row, sullen and defiant. I hated my staring classmates and I automatically hated Mr. Kelly because he was Authority, someone to be feared—like my stepmother, who terrorized my gentle father into indifference and bullied me into the life of a scullery maid after school.

Mine was an unrelieved, sordid existence of household drudgery. I had no friends because I was never free to play. Afraid of being pitied, I became a rebel and a lone wolf.

When life became absolutely unendurable, I would run away from home. Where does a twelve-year-old run away to in New York? Sometimes to the movies; oftentimes to walk unfamiliar streets or to sit in the park—all the while wishing you were dead because no one loves you.

My father was a violinist. Born in Russia, he had become an atheist, and I was raised without any religious education. Mother died when I was six months old; I was reared by friends until I was seven.

At that time my father married again and took me to live with him. Soon there was a new half-sister and then a half-brother to care for. I became their nursemaid, in addition to making beds, ironing, and washing. Once a week, on Friday, my stepmother would conduct a rigorous house cleaning. I would be forced to scrub the floor while she sat on a chair in back of me. Not until part of the floor had been scrubbed and rinsed five times, to her

complete satisfaction, would she move the chair back a few feet
so I could scrub the next section.

My father never remonstrated with her in this treatment of me.

Feeling rejected and unloved, I used to take my lunch to
school and while most of my classmates were at home, I'd munch
on a peanut butter sandwich and read at my desk. For one lovely
hour I'd retreat into the only world that gave me pleasure.

One noon, about two weeks after I entered Mr. Kelly's class,
he had lunch at his desk also. We didn't exchange a word,
though I was acutely conscious of that bony, red-haired Authority across the room. We shared the room in silence for over a
week, then Mr. Kelly offered me a glass of milk. Another day it
would be a piece of fruit, or a fried chicken leg—"extras," as he
put it.

After several days of gulping down these unaccustomed delica-
cies, I suddenly turned on him:

"You keep your old food! I don't want your pity."

"Pity!" he exclaimed, walking back to his desk. "And why, for
heaven's sake, should I pity you? You're bright and you're
pretty—and I like you."

That night I stared at myself in the mirror. A thin, unhappy
face with enormous green eyes and stringy yellow hair stared
back at me. Mr. Kelly, I decided, was a liar and not to be trusted.

A few days later my father told me that an aunt was sending
me a piano she no longer needed. I was delirious with excitement. But a week went by and no piano. And finally my father
told me my stepmother refused to have it in the house.

"And you let her?" I cried, sick with disappointment.

I thought of the skates I never got, the birthday cake I wanted,
the free time I begged for to join the Girl Scouts—all promised,

and all undelivered like the piano. I hurled wild, angry accusations at my father, and for the first time he whipped me.

I ran out the door, down five flights, and kept running as though escape could remove me from my father's betrayal.

I slept on a strange roof that night and as soon as it was light I went out to Bronx Park. By noon I had been turned over to a truant officer.

Trembling with fear, I was marched into Mr. Kelly's classroom. But before I could speak, Mr. Kelly dismissed the class for library study.

And then we were alone.

"I saved some milk for you."

"You mean you're not going to punish me?"

"I'm afraid you have it all wrong. You've punished me—by running away."

"But I didn't run away from you," I protested.

"I know, but if you liked me, you'd treat me as a friend and tell me your troubles."

"Oh, but I *do* like you," I said with awful urgency.

"Good," he said. "Now, how about that glass of milk?"

After that day I stopped running away because I now had Mr. Kelly to run to. Yet, I still used to storm at Mr. Kelly because he wouldn't share my anger over the latest injustices at home.

"It will pass, child," he'd say, his blue eyes luminous with affection and sympathy. "Believe me, it will pass if you'll stop hating and start being nice to people."

It was too big a step then, but time and again, during hostile exchanges with my stepmother, I'd suddenly stop my own hot torrent of words and remember Mr. Kelly's gentle admonishments.

"Don't hate, child. Please don't hate. Not even unkind people.

Remember the Master's words: 'Love your enemies, bless them that curse you, do good to them that hate you.' "[4]

"But, Mr. Kelly—"

"If you spend all your time hating," Mr. Kelly said, "you will have no time to like yourself. If you like yourself, you'll want to do things that are good."

Gradually I stopped dreading each new day and, in an effort to please Mr. Kelly, I began to take an interest in my studies and in my appearance. I wore a fresh middy blouse every day, which I washed and ironed myself, and took a bath every night. I won an inner battle by ignoring my stepmother's sarcastic comments on my new fastidiousness.

Mr. Kelly never commented on my clean, new appearance, but his blue eyes twinkled with approval.

Our lunch hours underwent a subtle change. I now listened to Mr. Kelly. And I began to comprehend his reiteration:

"Be good to yourself. Start liking people."

"My stepmother, too?" I challenged on one occasion.

"Well," he said, grinning delightfully, "the saints would approve."

The room rang with the rare sound of my own happy laughter over a shared joke.

The more I relinquished hatred as a way of life, the easier it was to shed my crippling fear of rejection. In the course of time I began to have friends—especially Hilda and Jean.

That year Hilda and Jean and I planned to spend Easter Sunday together and at supper, a week before Easter, I asked my father if I could have a new Easter outfit. "Easter outfit," my stepmother snorted. "What next?"

"All my friends have them," I said. "Why can't I?"

[4]*Matthew 5:44*

"There is no money for that nonsense," she said.

I felt a rising wave of helpless anger. I closed my eyes and counted to ten (as Mr. Kelly had told me to do) and when the anger passed, I said to my father:

"That's not fair. The younger children have new clothes and she has a new suit."

Without warning, my ears rang under the sudden hard crack of my stepmother's hand against my face. I blinked back the quick spurt of tears and got up.

"You treat me like a servant," I said quietly. "From now on you'll have to pay me like one. Starting this week I'm charging 50 cents for scrubbing the floor." Then I left the table and went to my room.

I did not get a new Easter outfit, but I received a far more important gift. I had regained my self-respect.

"It will pass," Mr. Kelly had said. And it did. That evening spelled the end of my serfdom. My life didn't become easy, but it was infinitely better. And from then on I was obsessed with the desire to pay a debt of gratitude to Mr. Kelly. It took a year and a half of hard study and careful planning before I could do it. And then the day came. The big assembly hall was filled with the parents of students graduating from eighth grade. It didn't matter that my father said he'd try to come and didn't, or that I had no flowers. I had Mr. Kelly whose belief in me was my greatest gift—and now I was able to return his gift of love in the only manner deserving of it.

I told the story of Mr. Kelly in my valedictory address.

Lola Kovener

Lola Kovener wrote for inspirational magazines during the second half of the twentieth century.

NUMBER NINE
SCHOOLHOUSE

R. Lovewell

Miss Malvina was nostalgic that particular September morning. More and more, her thoughts had to do with the past, the years when she was needed and when she was making a difference in people's lives, there as schoolmistress in Number Nine Schoolhouse. Now the dear old schoolhouse was empty—only memories remained within. She must go there to be with them.

onder why the doctors haven't ever been smart enough to think up some way to cut out whatever 'tis women cry with, Malvina Marean considered as she listened to the sound of spasmodic sobs in the room behind her.

She had come out on the piazza and was prepared to rock patiently until Mary dried her tears. *'Twould certainly save a sight of trouble in the world if women weren't able to cry. Crying always riles men up. Wonder what they would do if they couldn't bawl once in so often. Men take it out in hollering their heads off or having dumb spells or something else. But women cry. All that started Mary off was Sam's never saying a word about that lemon pie she took such pains with. 'Twouldn't have hurt him a mite, either, to have said it was good, but that's the man of it. They don't see the need of praising a woman's cook-ing—think they ought to be satisfied if what they bake is eaten. Oh, well, they'll get over it. First year after young folks get married there's bound to be some spats—always are, I guess.*

Miss Malvina lived in two upstairs rooms in the house with Mary and Sam, who were her next of kin. And her last of kin. Part of the place was hers, the rest Sam had inherited.

She squinted near-sightedly up the yellow dirt road toward the village. In a moment the school truck rattled into sight packed with noisy youngsters swinging school books and dinner pails. She waved her hand as the truck flew by, watching it go down the hill past the white schoolhouse, Number Nine. Before the town voted to transport all the children to the Center, Miss Malvina had taught there many years. Now that she taught no more, the sturdy deserted old structure seemed to her like a friend, a companion. The key to Number Nine was inside the clock in her kitchen, and every few weeks she went down the hill and sat for a while at the desk which had so long been hers.

The one skeleton in the closet of her peaceful life was the fear that the town would tear it down or move it away.

A consuming longing to go back across the years possessed her. She wanted, torturingly, to teach school again just for a day. She had little to do now—only to make her bed in the morning, to putter with the family mending, to sit in the sun and dream.

Mary came out to feed the hens. Watching, Miss Malvina saw Sam slip from the barn and join her, saw his arm go 'round her shoulders, Mary's yellow head drawn close under his chin. She was glad they had made up; but, some way, the pretty thing she had seen only made her more lonely, shutting her out completely from their united lives. She pulled herself from the rocking chair, went indoors, put on her hat and cape, took the schoolhouse key from the clock, and started down the road.

❧

She was so deep in her dreams in the old schoolhouse that she did not hear the purring of the car that had halted outside. But footsteps in the entry startled her and she looked up to find a man standing on the threshold.

"Miss Marean!" he cried. "Well, what do you know about this? I didn't expect to find you still on the job." His twinkling dark eyes awakened vague, faraway memories of a little boy with a freckled nose.

"I was driving up this way on a trip to the White Mountains and I thought I'd swing through the old town. I was going to hunt you up, but I saw the door open and had to stop and take a look. Say," he went on to her with outstretched hand, "it's great to see you; but I don't believe you know who I am."

"You're little Joe Becker. And you used to have to sit up in front where I could watch all your cutting up."

"Little Joe is good!" he laughed. "Weighed myself this morning—225 pounds." The visitor sat down on the platform at the old woman's feet. "You kept me after school pretty often, Miss Marean," he accused.

"And made you spat the erasers to get the chalk out. That wasn't much of a punishment, though, after the way you used to cut up—throwing spit balls and such mischief. I never once supposed you'd ever grow to be such a whopping big man. You were such a skinny fellow. I'd lost all track of you, too. Where do you make your home, and what business are you in?"

"I live in New York, and, well, I don't have to work much now. My business has prospered, and I've made quite a lot of money. . . . Say, I can see old Bill French up in the back seat wrestling with cube root. Wonder where he lives now."

"I don't know as I know myself. But it was fun teaching cube root—getting the answers to come out right."

Becker gazed for a moment out over the desks in the schoolroom. "Do you know what ever became of Sadie Davis?" he asked slowly.

"I've lost track of her too, Joe. She went off to work someplace and never came back. Seems as if I've heard she was married. But it was so long ago I've almost forgotten. I suppose you're married and have a family?"

"Yes, two boys and a girl. My, but I wish I had sent them out here for you to teach. They've been to the most expensive schools in the country and they can't add a column of figures straight to save their necks."

"But I'm not teaching any more, Joe. I'm only just sitting here. This school's been closed going on five years. Let's see. I'm almost seventy. I taught up until I was sixty-five—that makes it longer than I thought. The school committee didn't dare to put me out. Had to shut up the schoolhouse in order to get rid of me." She chuckled and a twinkle came into her blue Yankee eyes.

"I can't seem to remember the year we moved to Boston," Joe said reminiscently. "I was only a little shaver then."

Miss Malvina bent over the desk. "I shouldn't wonder if the register is down in the bottom drawer. Maybe it's the one you're in." Hunting, she found it. "In September 1885 there was entered the name of Joseph T. Becker, aged thirteen. Look at all the tardy marks after your name. You gave me considerable trouble as I recollect it. Here's the Davis girl's name. She was eleven years old. I kind of suspected you were sweet on her, weren't you?"

The big man grinned, rose, and went down the aisle, flung up a desk cover, and studied it for a moment. Cut deep in the wood were the initials J. B. and S. D.

"Funny how I remember whittling them out with a jackknife. Just popped into my head like a flash."

❦

For weeks Malvina Marean talked and dreamed of Joe Becker's visit. On the afternoon of Labor Day she heard a knocking at the front door and a man's voice speaking her name. The voice had a familiar sound. In a moment Mary came tearing up the stairs and rushed, bright-eyed, into the room.

"Aunt Malvina, you're wanted. Do you feel well enough to get up and take a little ride? Wear your new dress. That Mr. Becker who was here a while ago has come back."

Miss Malvina was so flustered that she didn't even notice which way they were going, until the car stopped right in front of the schoolhouse. She looked out then and saw long rows of cars parked beside the roadway.

"What's going on? Must be they've sold the schoolhouse."

"Just you come and see what's going on," Becker told her as he helped her out. Keeping his arm about her, he led her into the entry. And there, crowding the aisles and seats, were fifty or sixty men and women. On her desk were piled letters and telegrams. A great bunch of American Beauty roses greeted her misting eyes.

"Why, what—" She recognized a woman with gray hair. "You haven't changed a particle. You look just the same as you did when you were a little girl, Lucy Mann." They pressed forward to shake hands, her old pupils of the years that were gone.

"It's you who haven't changed," said Lucy Mann. "There never was a teacher like you in the world, and I don't believe there ever will be again!"

One by one they reported: Sadie Davis; Lewis Hallock from Chicago; Jessie Joslin who had never married; Mary Briggs who had six children; Sam, her brother, had died—he had been a great surgeon. *Always was doctoring animals,* Malvina remembered. The Harwell boys were out in California. They had sent their telegrams.

"I don't see for the life of me how you ever found them all, Joe. They have scattered to so many places, and live so far off."

"That was easy enough. I took along the register when I was here in June." He did not add that he had put three men to work tracing down every name—and that no one but himself knew the money it had cost to stage that reunion.

It was he who presented the loving cup her pupils had bought, a shining thing from a famous Fifth Avenue shop. "Malvina Marean" was engraved upon its side, with an inscription beneath which cut itself deep into her heart.

When they called upon her for a speech and she stood up behind the battered desk—her thin hands grasping the silver cup, their blue veins puffed and swollen with the years, her gaunt old figure trembling—the crowded room became suddenly very still. The roughened face of Sadie Davis softened to tenderness and Joe Becker's eyes were full of tears.

But Miss Malvina could not speak. Words would not come. A moment or two she stood, looking down at the men and women seated upon the school benches. Then she bowed her silvery head and shut her eyes. As she had "opened school" times without number, so now she would close it—for the last time.

"Our Father, which art in heaven—" her voice came tremulously. "Hallowed be Thy name—"

When the shortening September day had ended, the depot bus took its load away in time for the down-town train. The other cars started one by one. Miss Marean would not let anyone take her up the hill.

"I'm just going to sit here a spell," she told them. "I want to think it all over by myself."

Mary and Sam came back, after a while, and looked in at the window. But when they saw her sitting happily at the old desk, piled high with telegrams and letters that it would take a day to read, they went softly away without disturbing her.

No longer did Miss Malvina feel alone in the world. These strange men and women had by no means forgotten her. What did it matter now if she could not teach any more, if there was nothing left to do but sit in the sun and dream? Her arm brushed against the great loving cup, tipping it over, and she saw that there was a piece of paper inside it. She pulled out a long legal document. Unfolding the paper, her astonished eyes saw that it was a deed: the deed to the schoolhouse, Number Nine, made out to her—and then she was weeping.

"I guess the dear Lord knew what He was doin' when He made folks so they could cry. 'Twould be a terrible pity if they couldn't when they feel the way I do."

R. Lovewell

Nothing is known today of R. Lovewell.

GIRLS WILL BE GIRLS

Patricia Sherlock

It was yearbook dedication day. But it would be no contest. Most likely it would go to "No Problem" Walter J. Flynn—no matter what the problem or excuse, he made it easy. Now teachers like Miss Alexander who were tough—no way they'd ever be so honored.

And so it was once again.

*W*e were young and thoughtless. We had yet to learn that other people had different hopes and dreams and needs.

❧

Sitting in the auditorium that day, we—the senior class of Williamsport High School—had gathered for our last assembly before graduation to dedicate our yearbook to the teacher of our choice. We were a noisy lot and Bill McLaughlin, our class president, asked us to quiet down, with a special look toward our row of girls.

Most of the teachers were seated toward the back of the auditorium, but one teacher, Miss Mercedes Alexander, sat where she always did, at the very end of the aisle in the sixth row, ready to pounce in any direction as she saw fit.

I nudged my best friend, Rose. "You'd think she'd let up for the last assembly."

"Are you kidding?" Rose asked. "After what the old battle-ax did to us?"

Looking over at Miss Alexander, I remembered and it still hurt. Battle-ax was right!

Bill held up the yearbook, hoping to quiet us down, but a loud roar went up instead. Rose and I were on the yearbook staff so we knew who would get the dedication. For the third time in twelve years it was going to Walter J. Flynn, known affectionately as No Problem. For no matter what troubles you brought to him, those were usually the first words he spoke.

Forget your lunch money, fail a test, lose your homework, the answer never varied: "No problem!" Mr. Flynn went out of his way to make things easier. He was a nice teacher who could soften any blow, and nice teachers got yearbook dedications.

". . . so as we end one part of our lives and embark on another, we wish to show our appreciation to this fine—"

"Why is Bill taking so long?" I asked Rose. "He's really milking it." I grew restless and began looking around. In a class with more than three hundred students, it was impossible to know them all. Yet when I realized I'd never again see many of them after next week, I felt sad. There was only one face I knew I would not miss: the one on Aisle G.

Miss Alexander, having conceded that spring had arrived, had discarded her long-sleeved crepe blouses for ones with short sleeves. We had figured out her entire wardrobe as we sat in her World History II class that year. It wasn't much. There were five basic tweed skirts, three long-sleeved crepe blouses, three cardigan sweater sets, and one white silk blouse which always was worn with the lumpy, shapeless jacket to one of the tweed skirts.

Because all her clothes seemed to be in shades of tan, beige, and brown, we nicknamed her Mother Earth. She wore brown tie oxfords that matched the worn leather briefcase she carried. In the winter, she wore a shapeless brown coat and a knit cap which she pulled over her ears.

She had been teaching for almost forty years, which meant she had begun the year before my mother was born. Her hair, done in an old-fashioned way, reminded me of pictures I had seen of my grandmother. But, unlike Gran, Miss Alexander was not very pretty. Her nose was rather sharp and her lips were tight and rigid. Perhaps she had long ago given up on trying to do anything about her looks.

Even though she was well into her sixties, she was tall and ramrod straight. Her skin seemed stretched over her lean frame, giving it a translucent quality. But her eyes! Until recently, when I had come to dislike her so, I had thought Miss Alexander had eyes more beautiful than any I had ever seen. They were so clear they made an unclouded sky appear gray by comparison.

The strangest thing of all about Miss Alexander, though, was her voice. It was slow and rasping—what one of the girls described as "like someone long dead brought again to life." There was even a story to explain it. According to Williamsport legend, Miss Alexander—hard as it was to believe—had in her youth been a great beauty, friendly and outgoing, not at all like the stern and unsmiling woman she had become. She had been engaged. One day, she and her fiancé were out canoeing with Miss Alexander's younger sister. Suddenly the canoe capsized, throwing everyone into the water. When the story was first told, Miss Alexander had been a good swimmer. By the time it reached our generation, she had become some kind of Olympic champion. Anyway, Miss Alexander's fiancé could not swim, nor could her sister.

Thus, in one heart-rending moment, she had to decide which one to save. Blood being thicker than water, Miss Alexander chose her sister. The young man drowned. In grief and despair, she lost her voice. It took months for her to learn to speak again, and when she did, that was what her voice had become.

At the end of my junior year, I learned I'd have Miss Alexander the following term. Despite what I'd heard, I was determined to do well in her class no matter how eccentric she was.

I was not prepared then for our first encounter. She was standing in the doorway of her classroom that first day. I smiled at her as I tried to pass, but I was wearing a full skirt with three stiff crinolines underneath and I could not squeeze by.

"Good heavens!" she crackled at me with annoyance. "Why is your skirt like that?"

"The crinolines," I grinned, "I starch them in sugar and flour. That's what makes them so stiff."

"Imagine," she said, "wasting good food when people are starving." She gave a disapproving cluck and said, "Who are you?"

I didn't know anybody who was starving but I didn't think I'd better tell her that. "My name is Meg Reilly."

"Well, Margaret, I call that a senseless outfit for a schoolgirl. How do you expect to fit behind a desk." It was not a question. It was a statement.

※

By the end of that first class we all knew what we were in for. Until then, we had always been able to delude our teachers. All it took was discovering their vulnerability. With Mr. Almstead, the football coach, for instance, all you had to do in his biology class was get him talking about a play in Saturday's football game and he'd spend half an hour explaining it and never get around to giving the quiz he had scheduled.

It would not be easy pulling the wool over Miss Alexander's eyes. I remember the first time someone tried. Mike Klein had not done an assigned report and tried to soft-soap her. She cut him down like a Christmas tree in December.

Miss Alexander was fanatical about wildlife, nature, and fresh air. Mike's strategy was to get her going on some of the old trees on the school property, hopefully forgetting his report. He raised his hand and, eyes wide in feigned interest, asked, "Uh, Miss Alexander . . . can you tell me something about that giant tree by the Godwin Street entrance? I can't figure out what species it is. Do you know?"

"Do you mean, Michael, the one that is all carved with initials?"

"Yes, that's the one," and he winked at the girl next to him.

"Fools' initials in fools' places," Miss Alexander growled. "That happens to be a catalpa tree. It's been standing there nearly seventy-five years and now it's been so desecrated by idiots peeling away its bark, it's in danger of dying. Do you know why, Michael?"

"No!" Mike shot back, thankful his initials were not on the tree.

"Well, suppose you do a report for us explaining what happens to trees that are butchered. Now, let's get to your report on Benjamin Disraeli."

None of us tried that again on Miss Alexander.

When winter came, we were to find out how much Miss Alexander truly did love fresh air. Regardless of the weather, several windows remained open. There were times when snow drifted in the windows and melted on the radiators. We brought in notes from parents; we wore our coats. It made no difference. "Stagnant air leads to stagnant minds," she told us daily.

It was not uncommon to see her pulling her shopping cart along Main Street on Saturday afternoons. We tried to dodge her, but once in a while she would spy a teenager dropping paper on the sidewalk. She would walk over, pick it up, hand the litter to the villain, and escort him or her to a trash can. It was a one-woman campaign against litterbugs.

She wasn't so bad really and I almost could have liked her if it weren't for the fact that I could not get an A in her class. I had straight A's in every other subject and had been nominated for the National Honor Society, but every test I took for Miss Alexander came back with a B grade. And neatly penciled in the margins were her comments: "What does this mean?"; "Are you sure of this? Back it up"; "You have not developed this thought thoroughly"; and always, always, "I know you are capable of doing better than this."

Then it happened—in March. She was giving one of her spot quizzes when Rose leaned over and whispered, "Help! I didn't get to study last night."

I nodded and kept my left hand on my lap during the quiz.

The next day, Miss Alexander asked us both to remain after class. She showed us our quiz marks in her ledger. We both had F's.

"I am disappointed in both of you," she began. "The person who permits cheating is no less guilty than the one who copies." Then silence. She walked toward the blackboard, then turned and looked out the window. She was quiet for a very long time. Finally she turned around. "It pains me to do this, Rose and Margaret, but I must report this to the National Honor Society committee and have both your names removed. You no longer qualify."

My face was burning. It was not losing membership in the society that bothered me as much as the knowledge that everyone—my parents, teachers, friends—would know why I was disqualified. And it was all so out of proportion. Everybody cheated once in a while. I knew kids who were going to make the Honor Society who cheated. But they hadn't been caught. That was the only difference.

She was still talking. "If I pretend this did not happen, then I am guilty of cheating too. I will not do that, girls. I'm sorry." Her voice softened.

"The world will not end, you know. It is not so terrible to make a mistake, only terrible not to learn from it."

She was being conciliatory and I would have none of it. Tears stung my eyes but I would not give her the satisfaction of seeing me cry. Twelve years ruined by one crummy teacher! A lump so big I could not swallow it or bring it up caught in my throat. I ran blindly into the girls' room, spitting words out to no one at all. "That awful, hateful, spiteful old hag!"

The rest of the year in her class, I spoke only when spoken to, completed my assignments and tried to convey to her with my eyes the thought that I now considered her the lowest form of life I'd ever met. If she got my message, she never let on.

At last Bill was getting ready to name the teacher of the year. I was still watching Miss Alexander and so it was that I witnessed her momentary transformation. Her knuckles were gripping the cast-iron arms of her seat so tightly I could see the white of her bones. She was sitting up straight and a half-smile played on her lips. Her clear eyes almost danced in some kind of anticipation. But anticipation of what?

And then I knew. She was anticipating something that had not come to her in forty years of teaching, something that was not to come now and, in fact, probably never would—a yearbook dedication.

Impossible as it was, Miss Alexander was sitting there hoping to be named the most popular teacher in the school. Incredible! And for a moment, despite what she had done to Rose and me, something in the way she looked made me forget my hurt and feel hers.

". . . Mr. Walter J. Flynn, our teacher of the year!" Bill announced, and the place went wild. Miss Alexander released her grip on the chair and slipped back every so slowly. She pursed her lips and in a few seconds was applauding with everyone else.

In that brief moment I had glimpsed her vulnerability and

crossed the fine line between hate and love. But I had been vulnerable too and she had hurt me. Now I saw a way to hurt her back.

On the way home, I told Rose my idea. "Let's make a yearbook for Miss Alexander. I'll write a dedication and we'll get all the kids in our class to put their pictures in and sign it."

"That's crazy," she said. "Why should we do a thing like that?"

"Because she wants to be teacher of the year and when we give her a dinky little scrapbook, it'll point up how much we all hate her."

The next afternoon we went to the principal to see if he could give us a picture of Miss Alexander to put in the book. "It's a wonderful idea," he said, genuinely pleased, and gave us Miss Alexander's latest picture from her file. The next stop was the stationery store where we bought their ugliest and cheapest scrapbook.

The other kids in our class who had complained about Miss Alexander all year also thought it was a good idea and eagerly gave us their pictures. And when the students in her other classes heard about it, they asked if they could be included too.

When all the pictures were pasted in, I wrote the dedication, choosing the words with double-meaning mimicry. Finally, it was the last day of school. We were all seated and Miss Alexander began to ramble in her rasping voice about the sad state of the textbooks we'd turned in.

"Excuse me, Miss Alexander," I said, walking to the front of the room. "We—all of us—have something for you."

Miss Alexander looked bewildered and very suspicious. "Something for *me?*"

"Yes," I smiled. I took a deep breath and began reading.

"Miss Alexander, you have helped us all when we were cocksure no help was needed. You have taught us to love all of nature, the great outdoors, the sun, the snow, fresh air. You have impressed on us the sin of wastefulness and taught us that we should care enough for our fellow man to keep the world clean. You have taught us all year long that what we think is our best is never good enough. For all these reasons, Miss Alexander, we have chosen you our teacher of the year."

Miss Alexander looked stunned. I gave her the book and she began to leaf through it. "Why, you have my picture in here. Where did you get it?" And before anyone could answer, "Why, you're *all* in here," she said softly.

Then she put the book gently on her desk, removed her glasses and walked over to the windows. She did the same thing she did the day she knocked Rose and me off the National Honor Society. She stood there for a very long time.

All of us sat silently, not knowing what to expect next. After a while, she turned toward us. Her nose was red and tears were running down her cheeks. But she was smiling.

"Boys and girls," she said, her voice cracking more than usual, "you have made this the happiest day of my life."

I could not believe what I was hearing. Rose and I exchanged puzzled glances.

She dabbed at her nose with a hanky and went on, measuring her words carefully but filling them with an emotion none of us had ever suspected she possessed. "It has not been easy, you know, to be the kind of teacher I am. However, I have always believed that it was the best kind of teacher to be. I know," she paused and looked around kindly, "that I am not popular with students because of my standards. I know fun is made of me. Mother Earth—isn't that what I am called?" All of us cringed.

"Oh, it's all right. I'm used to it after forty years. Forty years." She said the number again, but more this time to herself than to us. "What's more important is that I have always tried to live up to my ideals, so that I can look at myself in the mirror and like the person I see.

"I know I have not been an easy teacher. My demands are high, but your abilities are also high. If I had expected less from you than I knew you could give, I would, in a very real sense, have been cheating all of you."

She had regained her composure and the tears on her cheeks were gone. Now there was a glow on her face none of us had ever seen before. In fact, she did not stop smiling for the rest of the class.

After school there was a faculty meeting in the cafeteria. The doors were open and as I cleaned out my locker nearby, the words I had written were being read by the principal. When he finished there was applause which lasted longer than any Mr. Flynn had received at the yearbook assembly the week before. I peeked in. Every teacher was standing to honor a beaming Miss Alexander.

I had purposely set out to hurt another human being. Yet somehow, in the tangle of events as they happened, that cruelty had been transformed by Miss Alexander's own goodness into a deep joy.

Now more than a decade later, the words of the dedication seem almost haunting. Over the subsequent years, what we considered Miss Alexander's crackpot views have proved to be uncannily prophetic: The Third World, pollution, wastefulness, environmental and ecological concerns. She used simpler words, of course, but those were simpler times.

But mostly when I think of Miss Alexander now, it is her own penciled message in the margin: *You can do better than this.* It is, I am still learning, not always easy to do better. There are times I don't even want to try, but the words have stuck as she must have hoped they would. And so, having become so much a part of me, it is a value I try to live by. I think that would please her.

It's strange, really. At the time, I thought there were so many teachers who were better. Now I know that none could compare to her.

Patricia Sherlock

Patricia Sherlock wrote for popular and family magazines during the second half of the twentieth century.

FATHER FLANAGAN'S
TOUGHEST CUSTOMER

Fulton Oursler

Father Flanagan had known some pretty tough customers in his Boys Town over the years. But never one to match this eight-year-old bank robber. Up till Eddie, he'd never been defeated by a boy. Every teacher on the place felt Flanagan had finally met his match.

Even Flanagan.

One winter night a long-distance call came to that Nebraska village known all over the world as Boys Town.

"Father Flanagan? This is Sheriff Hosey—from Virginia. Got room for another boy—immediately?"

"Where is he now?"

"In jail. He's a desperate character—robbed a bank, held up three stores with a revolver."

"How old is he?"

"Eight and a half."

The gaunt, blue-eyed priest stiffened at the telephone. "He's what?"

"Don't let his age fool you. He's all I said he was, and more. Will you take him off our hands?"

For years the Rev. Edward Joseph Flanagan had been taking unwanted boys off the hands of baffled society: youths of all ages, races, creeds.

"If I can't manage an eight-year-old by this time, I ought to quit," he said. "Bring him on!"

Three days later, Sheriff Hosey and his wife set down their prisoner in Father Flanagan's office—an unnaturally pale boy with a bundle under his arm. He was no higher than the desk. Frowzy hair of chocolate brown dangled over the pinched face; sullen brown eyes were half shut beneath long, dark lashes. From one side of his mouth a cigarette drooped at a theatrical angle. "Don't mind the smoking," pleaded the sheriff. "We had to bribe him with cigarettes."

The sheriff's wife laid a long envelope on the desk.

"There's a complete report," she snapped. "And that's not the half of it. This good-for-nothing criminal is not worth helping.

It's my personal opinion he ain't even human! Good-bye and good luck—you're going to need it!"

Now the heart of Father Flanagan was warmed by his love of God and man, and especially young ones. Looking upon this patched wraith of childhood, the priest thought that never had he seen such a mixture of the comical and the utterly squalid and tragic.

Waving the newcomer to a chair, Father Flanagan began to read the report. People had forgotten the boy's last name; he was just Eddie. Born in a slum near the Newport News docks, he had lost his mother and father in a flu epidemic before he was four. In water-front flats he was shunted from one family to another, living like a desperate animal.

Hardship sharpened his cunning and his will. At the age of eight he became the boss of a gang of boys, some nearly twice his age. Coached by older toughs of the neighborhood, Eddie browbeat them into petty crimes which he planned in detail.

About six months before the law caught up with him, his rule had been challenged by a new member of the gang.

"You never do anything yourself. You're no leader."

"I'll show you," replied Eddie. "I'll do something you wouldn't dare. I'm going to rob a bank."

The bank was housed in an old-fashioned building. When most of the clerks were at lunch, Eddie entered unseen and crossed to an unattended slot of the cashier cage. So small that he had to chin himself up, he thrust in one grimy paw, seized a packet of bills, and hid them in his jacket. Then he walked out to divide $200 among his comrades. But the exploit was a flop; the bank concealed the theft and there were no headlines.

"You're only cracking your jaw," the gang jeered. "You found that dough somewhere."

Eddie's answer was to disappear for several days. Someone had sold him a revolver, and he was out in the fields beyond town, practicing marksmanship.

This time the local front pages were full of him. Slouching into a restaurant at a quiet hour, he aimed his gun at the terrified counterman and was handed the day's take from the cash register. Next he dragged a roll of bills from the pocket of a quaking tailor. His third call was on an old lady who kept a candy store.

"Put that thing down," this grandmother cried, "before you hurt yourself!"

She smacked the gun out of his hand and grabbed him by the hair. Savagely he struggled; he might have killed her, but her screams brought policemen. Now Eddie had wound up in Boys Town.

᙭

Putting aside the report, Father Flanagan looked at the villain of the piece. In the dimmish light Eddie sat unmoving, head lowered, so that it was hard to see much of that sullen face. As the man watched, the child produced a cigarette paper and a sack of tobacco. With one hand, cowboy fashion, he deliberately rolled a cigarette and lit it, thumbnail to match. He blew a plume of smoke across the desk.

The long eyelashes lifted for a flash, to see how the priest was taking it.

"Eddie," began Flanagan, "you are welcome here. The whole place is run by the fellows, you know. Boy mayor. Boy city council. Boy chief of police."

"Where's the jail?" grunted Eddie.

"We haven't a jail. You are going to take a bath and then get supper. Tomorrow you start in school. You and I can become real friends—it's strictly up to you. Some day I hope I can take you to my heart. I know you're a good boy!"

The reply came in one shocking syllable.

About ten o'clock next morning Father Flanagan's office door opened and the new pupil swaggered in. His hair had been cut and neatly combed and he was clean. With an air of great unconcern he tossed on the desk a note from one of the teachers: "Dear Father Flanagan: We have heard you say a thousand times that there is no such thing as a bad boy. Would you mind telling me what you call this one?"

Back in the classroom Father Flanagan found the atmosphere tense. The teacher described how Eddie had sat quietly in his seat for about an hour; suddenly he began parading up and down the aisle, swearing like a longshoreman and throwing movable objects on the floor, finally pitching an inkwell which landed accurately on a plaster bust of Cicero.

Replacing Eddie in his seat, Father Flanagan apologized:

"It was my fault. I never told him he mustn't throw inkwells. The laws of Boys Town will, of course, be enforced with him, as with all the rest of us. But he has to learn them first. We must never forget that Eddie is a good boy."

"I am not!" screamed Eddie, cursing.

The child made no friends among boys or teachers. And for Father Flanagan he reserved his supreme insult—"a praying Christian." Spare time he spent roaming about stealthily, looking for a chance to run away. He stood aloof in the gymnasium and on baseball and football fields: "Kid stuff!" he muttered. Neither choir nor band could stir him; the farm bored him. And in all that first six months, not once a laugh or a tear. Soon the question in Boys Town was whether Father Flanagan had met his match at last.

"Does the little fellow learn anything?" he asked the sisters.

"Somehow he is getting his *ABCs*," they reported. "In fact he's learning more than he lets on. But he's just eaten up with hate."

This was not the first tough case Father Flanagan had dealt with. One youngster had shot his father, a wife-beater, through the heart. A murderer—but only because the lad loved his mother. When the priest had understood, he had been able to work things out. There must be something in Eddie, too, that could be worked out.

"I'll have to throw away the book of rules," grumbled Flanagan. "I'm going to try spoiling him—with love!"

Boys and teachers watched the new strategy as if it were a sporting contest, and the home team was Father Flanagan. Upon those weeks and months of planned treats the priest looks back with a reminiscent shudder: the scores of second-rate movies they sat through; the hot dogs and hamburgers, candy bars, ice cream and soft drinks that Eddie stuffed inside his puny body.

Yet never once did Eddie give a sign that anything was fun. In summer dawns that smelled of pines and wild clover, he would trudge stolidly down to the lake, but no grunt of excitement came when he landed a trout. An apathy settled upon him; he became more silent than ever.

Only once toward the end of that unhappy experiment did man and boy come closer together. At a street crossing in Omaha Eddie was looking in the wrong direction when a truck bore down on him; Father Flanagan yanked him out of harm's way. For one instant a light of gratitude flickered in the startled brown eyes, then the dark lashes fell again; he said nothing.

Even to the man of faith it began to seem that here was an inherent vileness beyond his reach. Hope had fallen to the lowest possible point when one soft spring morning Eddie appeared in the office, boldly announcing that he wanted to have it out with Father Flanagan. This time the brown eyes were glowing with indignation.

"You been trying to get around me," he began, "but now I'm wise to you. If you was on the level, I might have been a sucker, at that. I almost fell for your line. But last night I got to thinking it over and I see the joker in the whole thing—"

There was something terribly earnest and manful in Eddie now; this was not insolence but despair. With a stab of hope the priest noticed for the first time a quiver on the twisted lips.

"Father Flanagan, you're a phony!"

"You better prove that, Eddie—or shut up!"

"Okay! I just kicked a sister in the shins. Now what do you say?"

"I still say you are a good boy."

"What did I tell you? You keep on saying that lie and you know it's a lie. It can't be true. Don't that prove you're a phony?"

Dear Heavenly Father, this is his honest logic! How can I answer it? How can I defend my faith in him—and in You? Because it's now or never with Eddie—God, give me the grace to say the right thing.

Father Flanagan cleared his throat.

"Eddie, you're smart enough to know when a thing is really proved. What *is* a good boy? A good boy is an obedient boy. Right?"

"Yeah!"

"Always does what teachers tell him to do?"

"Yeah!"

"Well, that's all you've ever done, Eddie. The only trouble is that you had the wrong teachers—wharf toughs and corner bums. But you certainly obeyed them. You've done every wrong and rotten thing they taught you to do. If you would only obey the good teachers here in the same way, you'd be just fine!"

Those simple words of unarguable truth were like an exorcism, driving out devils from the room and cleansing the air. At first the tiny human enigma looked dumfounded. Then came a glisten of sheer, downright relief in the brown eyes, and he edged around the side of the sunlit desk. And with the very same relief Father Flanagan's soul was crying; he held out his arms and the child climbed into them and laid a tearful face against his heart.

That was a long time ago. For ten years Eddie remained in Boys Town. Then, well near the top of his class, he left to join the United States Marines. On blood-smeared beaches he won three promotions.

"His chest," boasted Father Flanagan, "is covered with decorations. Nothing strange about that, for he has plenty of courage. But God be praised for something else: he had the love of the men in his outfit—brother to the whole bunch. He is an upstanding Christian character. And still the toughest kid I ever knew!"

(Charles) Fulton Oursler
(1893–1952)

(Charles) Fulton Oursler, a Baltimore-born writer, journalist, screenwriter, and editor, cast a giant shadow over his age. Besides writing screenplays such as *Behold This Dreamer* (1927) and *All the King's Men* (1929), he wrote books such as *The Great Jasper* (1930), *The Greatest Story Ever Told* (a 1940 best-seller), and *Modern Parables*. He also edited *Metropolitan, Liberty,* and *Cosmopolitan,* and was senior editor of *The Reader's Digest.*

MATILDA

Mary E. Mitchell

*O*ne of our most common misperceptions in the field of teaching has to do with success-potential. We assume that top grades guarantee career success and low grades guarantee career failure. Professor Pillsbury belatedly learned that other qualities may be more significant than mere grades.

I'm sorry, Miss Haggett," said President Dacey. The sun, dropping to the west, shone full through the big window, slanting long, dusty beams across the president's desk. Matilda gazed dully at the scintillating motes which danced in the light, but nothing sparkling or lively had any message for her just then. She gave no sign, however, and stared so fixedly ahead of her that the president made a mental observation to the effect that the information he was imparting to Miss Haggett was not likely to disturb that stolid individual much.

"It cannot be a surprise to you," went on the president. "You were fully warned at the midyear examinations that your standard would have to be very much raised to allow you to graduate. We have done what we could for you through your course, but, some-how, you have failed to respond. Perhaps you have done your best?"

From the upward inflection, and the inquiring look on the speaker's face, Matilda felt that something was expected of her; so she answered, "Yes, sir."

"Well," continued the president, rapidly shifting his papers as if he could not stop working even to talk, "if you have honestly done your part, you have nothing with which to reproach your-self. Do not regret your time here. All you have learned will be of use to you, and there are many other paths in life besides that of a teacher. I don't suppose you will care to stay for graduation."

"No, sir," answered Matilda.

"Then I must bid you good-by, Miss Haggett, and repeat that I am heartily sorry we cannot grant you a diploma."

The president spoke kindly, but he went back to his work with the air of one who has finished an unpleasant duty. He became absorbed in the pile of documents before him, and hardly noticed that Miss Haggett left the room, or that Miss Pillsbury entered.

When the presence of his mathematics teacher did dawn upon his consciousness, he leaned back in his chair with a sigh.

"I've just disposed of Miss Haggett," he said. "She did not seem to regret the situation very much. I am afraid all the pushing and pulling we did in her case are thrown away. What do you make of her, Miss Pillsbury?"

Miss Pillsbury laughed. "Not a success in mathematics, at all events. She will be much more in keeping on her father's farm, feeding the hens and scrubbing floors."

When Matilda Haggett left the president's office, she felt that the end of the world had come—that is, the end of *her* world. Two years before she had entered the State Normal College with hopes high and happy, and now this was the end—failure.

She walked slowly away between the long lines of elms which shaded the campus path with their lofty, graceful branches. No one knew what those trees meant to that silent, awkward girl.

Then her thoughts went over the hills to her home by the quarry. She must go back and take up life again with its purpose gone. She could never be a teacher. Who would hire one who had failed to take her diploma? She wondered what the other girls had that she lacked. They did not study as hard as she, yet they had no trouble with their grades.

No more awkward or unattractive student had ever presented herself at Westlake College than Matilda Haggett. Her appearance was as unprepossessing as her name. The social life of the place was to her a mystery into which she never penetrated. She longed for it with all the strength of her shy nature, but she did not know how to make it hers. She loved the college, and it was to her as if she were banished from paradise when she packed her poor little wardrobe and bought her ticket home.

Matilda thought over the whole situation as she sat bolt upright on the car seat. Her mother would say that she was glad of it; the place for a girl was in the kitchen. Her father would grumble at the expense which had brought no return. There would be many questions asked and comments made all over the village, and the girl was not so stolid as she looked; she even winced at the thought.

It was a very wretched Matilda who climbed into the stage for Quarry Hill. Hanson Mires, the driver, slapped the reins on the back of his rusty old pair of horses as they started on their slow pull.

"Well, there, Tilly," he remarked, "I wasn't calculating to see you back quite so soon. Your pa told me you wouldn't be along for quite a spell yet. Ain't sick or anything?"

"No," said Matilda.

"Got your graduating, or whatever you call it done up before you expected, eh? I reckon you took all the prizes, now, didn't you, Matilda?"

A deep red mounted to Matilda's cheeks. Hanson was a diligent dealer in small news, but the truth might as well come out now as any time, and Matilda was not one to shirk.

"Oh, no, Mr. Mires," she said. "I'm home because I didn't pass."

"Didn't what?" inquired the merciless Hanson.

"Didn't pass my examinations. I've failed."

"Sho, now! You don't say so. Well, that's too bad. Better have stayed home in the first place, hadn't you?"

Matilda almost admitted in her heart that she had. She thought it again as she washed dishes that night in the hot, steamy little kitchen, under the fire of her mother's questions and her father's complaints, and it was forced upon her mind many times during the next few days, as she fell into her old place in the household. It was not the work Matilda minded. She gave to her domestic duties the same slow but faithful labor that she had expended upon her algebra. But the girl had taken a glimpse into another world, a world of thought, of gentleness and courtesy, of high aims and beautiful ideas. Would it be better to have remained ignorant of that world now that she could have no share in it? However it might appear to others, her heart answered, *No!*

Matilda's mind was busy with the question one bright September day as she sat on the rickety little back porch, shelling peas for dinner. Over the rock ledge that cropped out behind the house bobbed two little towheads, their owners busy at play.

Suddenly a shriek of infantile warfare broke the silence. Matilda put down her pan and went to the rescue. She separated the belligerents, shook them into good order, and returned to her work.

If there was something for them to do, they wouldn't fight so, she said to herself. *Those Peck twins are scratched up all the time, and they don't even know their letters. The Quarry Hill children are just going to the bad. If I had a diploma, I'd set up a school right away. Of course those babies can't walk all the way to Centerville.*

Here a pea intended for the pan took an erratic leap into space, impelled by a surprised action of Matilda's thumb as an idea seized her.

"Why!" she exclaimed aloud. "Why, I believe I will!"

❧

Nearly two years after that autumn day, Miss Pillsbury was sent out from Westlake on a tour of educational inspection. She visited large towns with their well-graded systems and imposing buildings, and small villages with their country schoolhouses. In both fields she found graduates of the Normal College doing good and acceptable work.

She was stopping in a mountain village in the western part of the state when she was told that three miles farther on there was a small settlement known as Quarry Hill.

"A forsaken place," said her informer. "They're a real wild lot up there, those quarrymen are. Foreigners most of them, and they don't care anything about learning. Some of their young ones used to walk down here every day, but it's a long tramp, and I believe they've got some kind of a school of their own now. You'd better not think of going, Miss Pillsbury; it's a rough road, and you won't find much."

Miss Pillsbury was tired. She had hoped to turn her face homeward that day, but instead she took passage in the stage for Quarry Hill.

Those struggling little schools are the very ones that need our help and encouragement, she said to herself.

The Quarry Hill schoolhouse was an old, unpainted barn. It stood upon the crest of a hill, and had for its outlook a whole world of rise and dip, of wooded slope and green valley, away to the purple mountains of the horizon.

Miss Pillsbury knocked at the rough entrance. A white-headed tot with a clean face and a ragged apron opened the door; then, abashed by the presence of a stranger, it introduced one stubby finger into its mouth and stared.

"What is it, Ingra?" asked a voice from within, and a young woman appeared, book in hand. The book fell to the floor as the young woman cried, "Miss Pillsbury!"

"Matilda Haggett!" exclaimed the visitor.

It was the rudest kind of a schoolroom, with its sagging floor and its unfinished walls. The desks were made of rough boards nailed onto crossed legs, and the benches were lower editions of the same. The children were of all sorts of ages. They looked happy, quiet, and docile.

"I hope you don't think it wrong of me," said Matilda, when she had dismissed her pupils to their recess.

"Wrong of you? I don't understand."

"Teaching without any diploma, Miss Pillsbury. It does seem presumptuous of me. I don't feel that I have any right to a school when I failed so; but this place does need it, and there isn't anyone else to do it. Of course I wouldn't take pay like a regular teacher."

"My dear Matilda," said Miss Pillsbury, "what do you mean? Are you not paid to do this work?"

"Oh, no; the children give enough to get some books. I couldn't take anything when they are so poor. You see, it isn't as if I were a real teacher, who had graduated."

"What do your parents think of such an arrangement?"

Matilda's face fell. "They don't like it much. Father says I've got to go earning next fall. I don't know what I shall do. There's a factory at Centerville, but I can't bear to leave here."

Miss Pillsbury looked at the girl before her in amazement. Could this be the stupid and unresponsive Matilda Haggett of the algebra class? Clumsy and plain as ever, and even more shabbily dressed, but she was actually dignified. When she spoke to her former teacher, she was the shy, awkward girl of old; when she confronted her scholars, there was no doubt but she was "Miss Haggett," absolute and supreme.

All that afternoon Miss Pillsbury watched Matilda and her

school closely. She made almost no comment on what she saw; but once she asked, "How did you learn to be so clear, Matilda?"

Matilda's answering flush was born of astonished delight.

"Do I make things clear? Oh, I am so glad, Miss Pillsbury! I don't know, unless it's because I have to study things myself, and I'm so stupid, you know."

Miss Pillsbury went back to the Westlake Normal College. At the first meeting of the faculty she gave an account of her journey. When she finished her report, she paused for a moment, then began to speak again, but not from her paper this time.

"I have yet to tell of a school," she said, "which, it seems to me, is accomplishing valuable and practical results. Beginning with five pupils in an ignorant and lawless community, it now numbers about thirty. The children, instead of running wild, are orderly and interested. The tone of the place has been changed. Some of the parents, who are foreigners, have formed an evening class, where they may learn to read and write. The teacher carries on her work, if not in accord with the latest pedagogical methods, at least with admirable simplicity and judgment. In humble circumstances herself, she gives her services. Her name is Matilda Haggett."

The president screwed up his eyebrows.

"Matilda Haggett! Was that not the girl who couldn't get her diploma?"

"The same Matilda," replied Miss Pillsbury, dropping her official manner. "The girl we all thought hopeless is working on in a humble, patient way, actually feeling guilty because she thinks she is not worthy to teach, apologizing to me for presuming to teach school without a diploma, yet, single-handedly making over the rough little village. And the most wonderful part of it all is that she really is a good teacher. She has to go down to the very bottom of things to understand them herself, and that is just what those children need. Of all the classes I visited, I enjoyed none more than I did Matilda Haggett's in that tumble-down shanty."

❧

It was graduation day at Westlake. Most of the students were from country towns and their families came by rail or stage, or drove in their own wagons to see their girls graduated. College Hall was well filled with an admiring audience of interested relatives and friends, and on one of the very front seats sat Matilda Haggett. She had come in response to a letter from Miss Pillsbury.

I want you to visit me during commencement week, and as I will not take no for an answer, I enclose a ticket for your journey. It will do you good to come, and perhaps you may get some points for your school.

Matilda winced as she read this last sentence. The thought of her school touched a sore spot. Her father had told her decidedly that when the summer was over, she must "quit playing" and go to work. Matilda admitted the justice of his decision, but her whole heart was in her school.

She shrank, too, from visiting the scene of her failure. But Miss Pillsbury's word was law to Matilda. She was too young and simple-minded not to be excited by the prospect; besides, there was the ticket! So once more she packed her trunk.

I'm so glad my best dress is all right, she thought, as she laid it in the tray. The "best dress" was a cheap muslin, bought two years before in happy anticipation of her own graduation. But in Matilda's eyes it was beautiful, and she spread out its clumsy folds with entire satisfaction as she took her seat in College Hall. Miss Pillsbury, with true delicacy, had made no suggestions in regard to the ungainly gown, but she had added a fresh ribbon here and a few flowers there, and had fluffed up the hair which, when allowed to curve into its natural waves, was Matilda's most attractive feature.

Matilda could not help feeling a pang of envy when the graduating class came on the platform, but she crushed it as unworthy. She listened to the exercises with great respect.

I never could have done it, she thought. *I wish one of them would teach in Quarry Hill. They'd know how so much better than I.*

President Dacey presented the diplomas with his usual felicity. *He's so handsome,* thought Matilda. *My, wouldn't I like to have him look at me that way, as if he was proud of me!* she added, in painful recollection of that dreadful day when she last stood in his little office.

"When a soldier in the British army distinguishes himself by special bravery," said President Dacey, "he is given a badge of honor called the Victoria Cross. It has no value in itself; no price can be set upon it. Its worth lies simply in its sentiment; it is the symbol of bravery. Like that plain iron cross, these certificates which I give you have no intrinsic value. They are of no possible use to you save in showing that you have honorably done your work. They are the 'Well done' pronounced upon your labor. It is with great pleasure that I have presented you with these diplomas. It is with *special gratification,* however, that I bestow one on a young lady, not a member of this class, but one who has earned it by faithful and successful endeavor. Will Miss Matilda Haggett please step up on the platform?"

"*I?*" responded Matilda, disbelievingly, from the front seat.

It took considerable pushing and encouragement and explanation to get the bewildered Matilda up on the platform. Finally she stood before the president, surprised out of her awkwardness into the simple dignity of perfect unconsciousness.

"I congratulate you heartily, Miss Haggett," said President Dacey, with his most stately bow.

And then Matilda, not knowing what else to do, broke down, and put her face in her hands and cried.

She cried once more that night, when Miss Pillsbury told her that an appropriation would be granted for the maintenance of a school at Quarry Hill, and that if she wished the position of teacher, it should be hers.

"You can earn quite as much as you could at the factory, Matilda," said Miss Pillsbury, "so I think you may feel certain that your father will be satisfied."

"But it doesn't seem right that I should have it," said Matilda. "I don't know a bit more about algebra than I did, Miss Pillsbury."

"Perhaps not, but you have learned a great deal about some other higher things," responded the teacher, as she tenderly kissed the girl good night.

Mary E. Mitchell

Mary E. Mitchell wrote for inspirational magazines during the first half of the twentieth century.

THE BOY WHO COULDN'T BE SAVED

Author Unknown

*B*uck Torres did it—he set the school on fire. No ifs, ands, or buts. Buck was through in the town; perhaps reform school would straighten him out.

Buck had but one defender: Miss Christie. One against the entire town—tough odds indeed! Tougher even than Miss Christie knew.

*T*hey told Miss Christie, "You can't do anything with riffraff like that." Why did she keep trying?

Now the school day was over. Five minutes ago the last footfall had echoed down the hall, the last harried teacher had turned in reports, but for Miss Christie Emerson, principal of Latimer Grammar School, the hardest job was still ahead. She was face to face with it this very moment, and she hadn't an idea how it was to be handled.

The boy sitting across the room was the school's problem boy. Miss Christie had taught for forty-three years, and this was the one pupil from whom she had failed to get some response. Although she was working on reports and not looking at him, she knew he was not looking at her either. He seldom met anyone's eye. He would be gazing straight ahead, that sneer on his face—almost a smile of satisfaction. Last night he had tried to set the schoolhouse on fire. Arson. A criminal offense. The evidence was nailed.

Miss Christie sighed. She had tried so hard to reach him, but now it was out of her hands. She could do nothing. They would turn him over to juvenile authorities for prosecution, and that meant the state reformatory.

Still without glancing up, Miss Christie spoke. "Buck, bring me the card index on that filing case, please." Her voice was detached, as if she were engrossed in her work. It was a trick she had used before. It eased the tension and it gave Miss Christie a little more time to think.

There was no movement in the room. She could picture the sneering response to her simple request, meaning *I'm not in your custody now. I'm big-time. Don't have to go to sissy school any longer. I'm a real character.* Then a foot scraped on the floor. Two feet. He shuffled across the room, slouched back, and dumped the box on the desk.

"Thank you. I'll be finished here in a few moments," she said conversationally.

It wasn't that she handled them with gloves—when Miss Christie pitched into a kid he remembered it—but she tried to treat a boy as if he were a responsible human being. She often said, "This is a grown-up world. The children can't understand our laws and attitudes, having had no adult experience, but they've got to abide by them. I'd like them to know why, if possible and to feel that they can depend on grownups for a square deal."

The door opened cautiously, and the old janitor stuck his head in. Then, not scenting too much brimstone, he retrieved the wastebasket and trotted hastily away. Miss Christie's pen scratched on. *I'd give my prize possession to escape this next half hour.*

Last night the town had been aroused by fire sirens, and Superintendent Clint had phoned Miss Christie after midnight. "We've had arson at your school."

"No!" There had been cases of vandalism, but arson—! "A fire? Do any damage?"

"Not much. The night watchman discovered it almost at once."

"But who would set the school on fire?"

Miss Christie hadn't slept a wink.

This morning Superintendent Clint came into her office early. "Well," he said, "we've got the culprit spotted. The night watchman had a good look at him as he ran. But we want conclusive evidence before we crack down . . ."

"It wasn't one of our boys, was it?"

"Yes, Buck Torres."

"Oh, no, not Buck!"

The superintendent said impatiently, "Who else? He's the troublemaker here, a chip off the old block. You can't do anything with riffraff like that."

Miss Christie said, "Was Kerbs sure?"

"Absolutely. The boy has even boasted about it."

"To whom?"

"Jimmy King. Mr. King came in this morning to tell us."

Miss Christie pressed her lips together. The Kings were well-to-do, prominent people and Jimmy was a little snob and a smart aleck.

"Have you spoken to Buck?"

"They had a dozen boys up for questioning; he was one of them. He clammed up of course."

Miss Christie thought fast. "Let me talk with him, Mr. Clint."

He frowned. "This is a serious matter. The town is panicked. They've stood enough from that Torres gang. People don't want their children in school with such like him, and they're right. Well, this will end it. I'm relieved to have enough on the boy to send him up."

"Give me one day, Mr. Clint," pleaded Miss Christie.

"It won't change matters. Why put it off?"

"I only want to hear Buck's version, not Jimmy King's."

He stood scowling, remembering that she always begged a second chance for the boys. "Well, all right—all right. One day, no longer. And I'll have to explain this to the chief."

All day Miss Christie had racked her brain. She had prayed. There was nothing one could say for Torres. His father had been killed in a police raid on a hide-out. His father's brothers were doing time for burglary. His stepmother, with whom he lived, was a drug addict. What chance had a fourteen-year-old boy, who had reached the fourth grade by staying in each class two years and then moved up via a social pass?

You couldn't make him study or cooperate. Pass his desk and you saw behind the arithmetic or geography a paperback or a sport sheet. Miss Christie always claimed that if a boy took an interest in one thing of merit, he was redeemable, and the hidden books were all on baseball. Once he had organized the little fellows into two teams. Every player had been named for a big-league star. Sauntering near, Miss Christie could hear him giving instructions:

"You there, Nelson Fox, you're covering second. You've caught the ball. Get your right foot on the base to put that man out; then whirl and throw to first to get that runner. See— this way." And to her surprise, the slouchy figure moved in a lightning-swift exhibition of skill that was pure grace and sureness. "It's as much the windup as the throw—you're Maglie. . . . Run in, Willie Mays; catch it backhanded. . . . Come on, Duke Snider. Put that ball over the fence. . . . You can't be a pitcher because you're left-handed? So is Joe Nuxhall."

Miss Christie was a little excited. Once, when a boy slid home safely, she clapped. Buck turned to discover her standing there, and flashed her a grin, another face shining through the sullen lines of his habitual face. But the parents soon discovered what was going on and had snatched their children away from the "bad influence." Buck had withdrawn into himself, reverting to the old don't-care slouch and the sneering responses. He walked to and from school alone, occasionally tangling with some tormenter. She had tried to talk with him about baseball but had received only muttered replies. He was suspicious of everyone, defiant and distrustful. But that one glimpse of a different look kept haunting her.

"Buck, come here."

He came and stood by the desk, looking straight ahead at the wall.

"Do you know anything about the fire?" Direct as a knife cut.

His eyes flickered. His feet shifted a little, and his shoulders moved. Then, "Naw."

Miss Christie pressed her lips together. "You haven't anything to tell me?"

The feet shifted again. She waited. Her face was stern, but her eyes held compassion. Buck's head came up. For a split second she thought he was going to talk. Then the curtain fell over the pinched features.

"Naw." Defiantly.

Miss Christie sat back in her chair. "Very well, Buck. You may go now."

He was taken by surprise. He had braced himself for a third degree. He must know that she was his one chance. Turning, he slouched across the room to the door. His shoulders sagged, and Miss Christie felt the sting of tears back of her eyes. Buck reached the door and put a hand out to swing it.

Miss Christie spoke more to herself than to him. "I'm sorry," she said, and her voice was weary. "You can't know how sorry. I've believed in you. You did things that troubled me. But there were other things—like helping the little fellows with their baseball team—I liked that. Well . . . ," she said, dismissing him.

He stood with his hand on the half-opened door, and Miss Christie went back to her reports.

He turned. She could scarcely believe it. He was coming back! Miss Christie didn't look up until he had been standing by her desk a little while. Then she raised her head and spoke gently, "Just the truth, Buck."

His voice was low and halting. "Jimmy King is always riding me about my old man and bragging about his dad's war medals and bravery. He'd tell me who all his ancestors were and what they did. He said George Washington was his great-great-great-granduncle, and who was mine, and I said Paul Revere. He said, 'Oh, yeah? Let's see you prove it. I bet you won't put a lantern in that tower at midnight.' We were on the bridge they're fixing near the school, and we both looked at the lanterns that would be lighted at night, and I said, 'O.K. You come back at midnight and I'll show you.' So he came. I picked up one of those lanterns and went in through a basement window and ran up to the tower. I'd meant to wave it at him and bring it back, but he's slippery. He'd say he didn't see it. So I looked around for something to set it on, and there wasn't anything up there but stacks of old papers as high as a man's head. I put the lantern up on a stack of papers and ran down right quick, and I said, 'You see it, don't you?' And he said, 'Ha, I got you! Paul Revere didn't put a lantern in a tower; he watched for it. You didn't even know. That proves you're a liar.' I was going to paste him one when he began jumping up and down and saying, 'Now you've set the schoolhouse afire.' And I looked, and the lantern must have turned over. The papers were blazing up. I started running back, and here come old Kerbs. So I scampered. I never meant to set anything on fire, Miss Christie. I was gonna put the lantern back where I found it. But won't anybody believe that."

"I believe it, Buck," she said. "I don't know just what I can do, but I'm going to work mighty hard. You see, it will be your word against the way you've been acting. Not what your father did. What he did can't really hurt you. Only you can hurt yourself. But I'm staying with you, and you've got to stay with me. Not let me down."

He had no graces of expression, and he could only stand there, head bent, fighting for control.

She said, "You go along home now."

"Yes, ma'am," he said humbly.

With the closing of the door, her sense of relief vanished into a gray fog of hopelessness. Buck might think that because she was principal here her word would carry weight, but Miss Christie knew better. It might even go against him. They called it Miss Christie's weakness. She always took up for the bad boys. Superintendent Clint had said she mothered them; a stern hand was what they needed. He had been emphasizing this recently. Miss Christie knew what he meant. She was getting old. Was he right? Did she handle them too gently? Too sympathetically? She thought not. Make too much of a child's fault and you implant that fault in his character.

Sitting here in the empty silent building, her thoughts went back, in an effort to gain from the past some course of action for the present. The years seemed to file through Miss Christie's heart in a troubled line of boys: of smoldering glances, sullen lips, shuffling feet, going out from here through this very door. To what? She had worked hard over them, but had it helped? Had it given them the chances they needed?

One case came back. She had been young then. Among her third-graders was an incorrigible Teddy Reynolds. When he got completely out of hand one day, she sent him to the principal with a note.

At recess she went down the hall to the principal's office. Opening the door, she stood shocked and horrified. Teddy cowered in a corner, a small bundle of quivering flesh. Above him, with a ruler in his hand, stood the principal, his face almost beyond recognition. He had completely lost control of himself.

"Miss Christie," he said in a voice shaken with rage, "he fought me like a tiger, cursed me. He's a little devil and I tried to kill him."

Oh, heavens, you almost have. The child has had a terrible beating.

"If he ever lifts a finger, bats an eye, send him back," the principal continued angrily. "The next time, I'll finish him." He scarcely knew what he was saying.

She was as sorry for the principal as she was for the boy, because normally he was an even-tempered man. Teddy must have given him a rough time. She left the room, sick at heart. Teddy was back in his place that afternoon, trying to hide his swollen face. When the closing gong sounded, Miss Christie said, "Now I've written something in this little book, and I want you to read it and think about it. Don't sign it unless you feel you can keep it."

She handed him a small black notebook in which she had written: "I, Teddy Reynolds, on my word of honor as a gentleman, do promise Miss Christie that I will try to obey the rules of the school."

After a time, the little book was shoved across the desk. Teddy Reynolds had signed his word of honor.

Afterward, if ever he got obstreperous, she had only to show him the little black book and catch his eye and smile. He stuck to his agreement, finished school, worked his way through college, and graduated with honors. And he had built a career in this town on his word of honor. It wasn't that Miss Christie had given it to him. She had only pointed out to him what he already had. You can bring out the devil in a child or his word of honor.

But what chance had this one misguided boy when the whole world was against him?

Again the door opened, and the old janitor, troubled, said, "Miss Christie, you goin' to sit here all night?"

She looked up, surprised that the room was growing shadowy. "No, John, I'm going now."

The eight-block walk home seemed extra long tonight. Every footfall was heavy. Fire-flies filled the soft April dusk, and somebody was broiling a steak. Miss Christie wished she had a steak, but she was too tired to fix more than a pot of tea and a sandwich. When she had finished her second cup, she went to the phone and called Jerry Fisher, young editor of the Latimer *Clarion*. Jerry had a crusading spot somewhere in his make-up, but he was down-to-earth, too.

"Jerry, can you drive out here tonight?"

"Funny thing is, I was practically on my way there. I want to talk to you."

Half an hour later, she heard his car on the driveway. "Well," said Jerry from the stoop, "there you sit brooding."

He had been a handsome boy when she taught him, and he still was.

"Jerry, I've got trouble."

He shot his finger at her. "It's no good, Miss Christie. We're better off without any embryo hoodlum. This town has really suffered from the Torres family, and personally I dread having another one grow up here. Already turning into a firebug. We're not safe."

"I've heard that a good many times in the past forty-three years about one boy or another. The town's still here."

"What I'm concerned with is you." He picked up a chair, turned it backward, straddled it, and eyed her solemnly. She wasn't a woman to quibble with. "They're gunning for you."

"Don't I know—"

"Well, then drop it. Let the authorities take over."

Miss Christie sat and considered. She was sixty-four. Almost at retirement age, unless she chose to go on. During the next few years, there would be other boys who would need her, if she stayed. Why throw away the needs of many for the need of one? But this boy. . . . She looked at Jerry and shook her head. "Are you siding with them, Jerry?"

"I'm just thinking of you. You'd feel pretty bad if they fired you."

"I'd feel worse if they sent Buck to Gatesville. Look, Jerry, are there records in your office or in the police files about the Torreses? I don't mean their criminal life, but family history."

"I can find out tomorrow."

"Do it tonight. I only have until tomorrow. One thing more; I want you to take me down where Buck lives."

"That's no part of town for a lady."

"I've got you with me."

He stood up, and paced the floor. "Have they phoned you tonight, the school board?"

"No."

"They're having a called meeting tomorrow morning. They say you're too easy on incorrigibles. They've got their eye on a man."

"Oh, no." Latimer Grammar was her school. She'd helped build the big new brick building in place of the old wooden one. Campaigned to get it sodded, an ice-water fountain, gymnasium, and playground apparatus. Fought every year for something new and needed.

Jerry was waiting, hands in pockets, troubled eyes on her. He'd hated to be the one to bring her this piece of news.

She looked up. "I can't drop it, Jerry."

"All right. Come on."

Step out under the stars. Sounds of distant music, lighted

windows, couples strolling, the happy shouts of children. Ordered, safe, and beautiful. God's world. A mile or so farther: a narrow dark alley, a stench from uncollected garbage, wooden shacks flush with the walk. Where are the stars now? This, too, is God's world.

"Do you know the house, Jerry?"

"Yes." And soon: "This is it."

They stopped. The place was totally dark.

"What d'you want?" a voice said almost at their elbow—a woman's voice, thick-tongued, drugged.

"Looking for Buck," said Jerry.

"He ain't here. Never here nights. Stays in that pool hall." The voice grew whiney. "Now don't you take Buck away. He's all I got to do for me."

They turned and walked back to the car.

Miss Christie said, "Go into every pool hall till you find him. See what he's up to."

"And leave you in the car alone?"

"I'll be all right."

Jerry was back in ten minutes. "Found him. He's glued to the radio, listening to the Giants–Dodgers game."

Miss Christie had what she wanted.

"Now you phone me later tonight, Jerry; no matter when," she admonished at parting.

"I'll do it."

❧

For years, life may go along with scarcely a ripple of change in the ordered routine of duties, work and pleasure. Then there comes a corner. Miss Christie had reached that corner today. She tried to pretend to herself that it was no more than many other crises in her forty-three years of teaching, but she knew better. She was old now. New methods had been established in other schools, and mostly she had stuck to the old ways. The world moves on. She drank her coffee, ate a little breakfast, and put on her best navy silk suit and a soft white blouse. She fluffed her hair about her temples. People are more likely to agree with you if you are not unpleasing to look at. Good of Jerry to tip her off about this called meeting.

The school secretary was already in the office when Miss Christie arrived. "Oh, hello, Miss Christie. You look spruce. They're having a meeting at 9:30 in the superintendent's office. They want you."

"Thanks, Jenny."

At 9:30 Miss Christie rose and walked down the hall to the superintendent's office, her heart pounding a little. She paused, her hand on the doorknob, feeling abruptly alone. Then she got the smile back on her face and went in.

The door opening startled a discussion that hushed away into almost embarrassed silence at her entrance. Seven men sat about the big table—six board members and Superintendent Clint. The chairman of the board was the town's banker. He sat at the head of the table, a serious middle-aged man with a poker face. To either side of him were superintendent Clint and the owner of the big textile mills, Richard Martin. Then Sid Seymore, a merchant; Olen Merriweather, president of the City Council; Jake Bevins, a lawyer; and the board's newest member, young Dr. Henderson.

Miss Christie mentally reviewed them. The banker would be difficult; he stood for the right as he saw it. Rich Martin headed the Rotary Club—a go-getter, genial and friendly. Sid Seymore would be with the banker. Olen Merriweather was a hard nut to crack, and Jake Bevins could be stubborn as an old field mule. Dr. Henderson, young and malleable, was her one hope. You have to be pretty old or else pretty young to understand life.

There was a chorus of good mornings, and Miss Christie sat down. The seven looked at her with a sort of helpless chagrin, the way men look at a woman when they know she's going to disagree with them.

The superintendent said, "This is an emergency meeting, Miss Christie, because this problem can't wait. If the boy is guilty—and I think we're all pretty well satisfied on that score—we want to turn him over to the juvenile authorities this morning. The town is seething with uneasiness, and they don't want him loose tonight. I suppose you didn't get anything out of him?"

"Yes," said Miss Christie, "I did. He told me the whole thing."

"Admitted it?" asked the banker, leaning forward.

"Well, yes."

Everyone sat back. Superintendent Clint sighed with relief, "A confession simplifies everything."

Miss Christie said, "That depends on what you call a confession, Mr. Clint. He told me what happened. Did it ever occur to you that Mr. King, who came to you with the tale, might be covering up for his own son?"

A smile went around the table. The Kings against this Torres brat? Superintendent Clint said, "The night watchman saw him."

"Yes, Buck put the lantern in the tower, but he didn't mean to set the school on fire." Leaning forward she told them Buck's story. Then she said, "If one boy is culpable, why aren't both of them?"

The lawyer, Bevins, raised a skeptical eyebrow; Richard Martin smiled amusedly; the banker looked at her from behind his business face; Dr. Henderson sat back in his chair, eyes narrowed thoughtfully. Not one of them believed Buck's story.

Then Superintendent Clint said, "Of course he'd make up something like that—trying to shift the blame. He isn't noted for veracity, is he? The boys know you're too soft-hearted and you'll always take their part. It's got to where they can pull off anything in your school, Miss Christie, and hide behind your skirts."

Sid Seymore spoke up. "We've talked with him—talked at him, and there's nothing there. The boy comes from low stock, steeped in crime from the cradle. Actually, all of us here are to blame for what occurred and what it might have grown into, because we've already overlooked so much other vandalism. We couldn't pin it on him before, but now we have something he can't squirm out of. I really don't see how you can say one word in his defense, Miss Christie. He set this building on fire!" His fist came down.

Miss Christie had the disadvantage of always seeing both sides. She saw her side now and she knew they were thinking, *We're always making concessions to Miss Christie and it simply can't go on.*

"Ever look in his face?" asked Olen Merriweather. "At that sneer?"

"He's defending himself the only way he knows how. What any boy needs is someone on his side. Do a wrong to a boy and he grows bitter and resentful; you make a criminal out of him. He's confessed his part, and we ought to give him a second chance."

"A chance to burn up another school?" Superintendent Clint exploded. "I want to go to sleep tonight knowing that the town is safe. Safe from that Torres gang."

"Yes, I agree we ought to do something about it," said Miss Christie with spirit. "We ought to have a playground in this town with equipment, baseball teams, a swimming pool, tennis courts. How much does it cost to keep a boy in the reformatory a year? Fifteen hundred dollars. How much better if that money could be spent to keep the boys busy and occupied. Develop their natural faculties. This boy is not a bad boy. I've had considerable experience and I know good material when I see it. Buck Torres is good material. He could be valuable. I've watched him for two years and I like what I've seen. He fights because the boys tease him. He takes care of that old woman out there, and he spends his evenings in the pool hall where he can listen to the baseball games. You say he's a Torres. Well, Jerry Fisher looked up the Torres family last night. Torres was not Buck's father."

She saw Dr. Henderson nod slightly, but her words glanced off the rest of them without even a dent. They had come there with their minds made up, agreed among themselves that they had let Miss Christie bulldoze them too long.

The bank president spoke. "Miss Christie, we appreciate your kind heart and your unfailing interest in the boys. But none of us are right all the time. And you aren't. It's taking chances not to lock this boy up—put him in a place where he'll learn respect for the property and rights of others. When he comes out—and if he goes straight—he can live a normal useful life and get a good job."

"In your bank?" asked Miss Christie. "Will you give him a job in your bank?"

The banker smiled, "Not by a long shot!" But he sobered quickly. "We've got a hard year ahead. The railroad is moving in twenty-five new families. Mixed nationalities. Some look pretty tough. Their kids will go to Latimer School. They'll be too much for you. Too much for any woman." He spoke kindly, but it had to be said: "You've carried the burden long enough. You've done wonderfully. All of us appreciate that. But now we need a man."

The room was very still. A rather uncomfortable stillness,

touched with relief. This was out in the open. Miss Christie was fired.

For just a moment she seemed to grow smaller, sitting there in the navy silk worn to impress them. After all her years of effort and labor, she wished the end might have been otherwise. Not eulogies, but honest regret and appreciation. "I'm sorry you're going. Good luck, Miss Christie." She had brought it on herself, of course. Miss Christie stood up. She had entered the room as employed by the city fathers. But now everything was changed. She was no longer beholden to anybody. She was free. And her freedom gave her a long perspective, a sense of distance. She looked down the table at them, and abruptly they were not the town's leading citizens but boys in school at various ages and in different years. She lifted her shoulders and held her head high. That old glint of steel came into her eyes. It made Miss Christie look taller.

"You don't need me at this meeting any longer, but before I go I want to ask you a question. Did any of you ever do anything when you were boys that might have turned into tragedy if someone hadn't taken your part? Think back. Every one of you." She pointed a finger at Richard Martin. "Rich," said Miss Christie sternly, in her well-remembered school teacher voice, "what about those broken windowpanes? Was that a high-spirited prank or vandalism?" The finger moved to Lawyer Bevins. "Jake, who was it who climbed the flagpole and took down the town's expensive new silk flag and hid it?"

His face turned red, but no one saw. Miss Christie had moved on to Merriweather. "Olen, a stolen car is something to laugh about now, but it might have been called plain theft. . . . Sid, who was it picked up a stone and threw it, and hit the principal on the arm? Just a small boy dare, and the principal knew it was, and

tossed the little pebble back. But it could have been called assault."
She looked at the bank president. "Reynolds, was there a time
when you needed—not a strong arm, you had that—but somebody to understand, to believe in you—to call out the best in
you?"

He sat transfixed.

"Just remember," said Miss Christie, "that what you do here in
the next hour will save a boy—or make a criminal."

She turned and started toward the door. But before she
reached it, there was a hurried step, then a hand was on her arm.
"Wait, Miss Christie." It was the bank president. "You're right.
We forget. There's something that is ageless. You've got it, and
we need it here in this school. We need you," he said gruffly.
"That recreation center—I'll make it a personal gift to the town."

Chairs scraped and through a blur she saw them surge toward
her, but the young doctor got there first.

꒰ꗥ꒱

Miss Christie was at her desk working on reports. The building
was quiet. The last boy had gone. The last but one. He sat on a
chair against the wall, awaiting the verdict.

Miss Christie looked up. "Buck, come here." She was smiling.

He shuffled over, stood dejectedly; his pale face a degree
whiter, the dingy cap twirling between unsteady hands.

"It's all right, Buck. They're going to take your word—to trust
you. Jimmy King was sorry he got you into all this trouble. He
came in with his father and they talked to the school board about
it. I think he'll be your friend now, Buck."

Too astonished to comprehend, he widened his eyes as they

came up to meet hers. And back of the astonishment she saw a wonderful thing bloom on a scared boy's face—hope.

Miss Christie fought a battle with a stubborn lump in her throat and won. "I have something else to tell you. I've been investigating, and we found that Jacques Torres was not your father. He took you when you were a baby. Well, that relieves you from any responsibility to his wife. Buck," she said briskly, "do you think you could build a shed—a room on the back of my house? I want to get a power mower and other garden tools so you can keep the yard pretty. We can enclose the screen porch for a room for you."

His face underwent a series of changes as each surprising sentence opened a new facet of life.

"You mean—?" he swallowed. "You mean I'm to live at your place?"

"At *our* place. You're to be my boy," said Miss Christie proudly. "I've had it in mind a long time, Buck. I need somebody. I'm not so young as I was."

She could see the muscles along his jaw jerk. His eyes were swimming, but they met hers squarely. And something passed between them so bright, so dazzling, that for a moment it seemed to light the room, and the town, and the whole world.

Then Buck spoke. His voice was gruff, but this time it had a ring: "Yes, ma'am!"

A LESSON IN
DISCIPLINE

Teresa Feley

They were the class from hell—or "Les Misérables."
No teacher had ever been able to control them.

Then came Miss Barracombie.

*W*e were a terrible class. Every class likes to remember that it was pure hellion, but the thirty of us who started under Miss Gallagher at the Down School near the Buick garage really were terrible. We came along just when the argument between the phonics people and the associationists was at its height. We went at reading for three years by the word-recognition method and then in the fourth grade the teacher insisted that we learn to read all over again by sounds. We were also caught in the controversy over manuscript and cursive writing. And we hit the crisis in arithmetic.

In the beginning of the fifth grade, we were forbidden to use brackets in finding the lowest common denominator. We had to go click-click to an equivalent fraction instead, seeing all the pieces of pie in our heads. This meant that nobody at home (after all, who had Gestaltists in their families?) could help us any more. But, willing sneaks, we drew brackets with furtive fingers on our pant legs.

Child-centered psychology burgeoned in our town at this time. We were allowed to do some ridiculous things in school because we wanted to. When our parents heard about them, they were furious at first. Then they decided that the school must know what it was doing, and they let us do the same things and worse at home.

Every year for six years we grew stupider and lazier and fresher and more obnoxious. No one ever separated any of us, or kept any of us back, or adulterated us with new blood. We were a terrible package, referred to by certain members of the PTA as "Les Misérables."

Then came the seventh year and Miss Barracombie.

She was new to the school that year, so we did not have the usual case studies on her from previous classes. Her looks might have given us a clue, but we had always known amateur, experimental teachers so we did not recognize the career teacher when we saw her. She was perhaps fifty, tall, square-shouldered, and erect; neither feminine nor mannish, merely healthy and strong. Her face was handsome but not pretty. She had no subtle expressions: she smiled outright, she frowned outright, or she concentrated. Her voice was not harsh but had a peculiar carrying quality, vibrating longer than most. Eugene Kent took off his hearing-aid after the first day.

She greeted us that day as no teacher ever had. No talk of adjustment here, no plea for growth, no challenge to find ourselves. She said:

"My name is Virginia Barracombie and it will be Miss Barracombie to you indefinitely. One of these days you will meet someone from the last school in which I taught. The worst that he tells you about me will be true. It's a far cry from child to man, and it's not through games that we get there. You and I are bound together in a contract for one year. I teach; you learn. Behave yourselves and pay attention and this will be one of the good years of your lives. You have a minute to prepare yourself with ruler, compass, pencil, and paper for a review of the meaning and use of decimals."

It was the shock treatment all right—but with economy, with the clarity of piano keys struck singly, above all with authority. We had neither the opportunity nor the mind to look across the aisles at each other until recess. We were at work in the first five minutes—we, who always had a period in which to get ready. It was a blow to our unit pride, but we were less cohesive after the long summer and temporarily distracted from getting together on what to do about it.

We thought at first that we were just going along with her in a momentary tolerance. She was a novelty, and among teachers that was hard to find.

Then we found ourselves bound in a work routine. At that point some of us tried to bolt.

In its reactions to Miss Barracombie the class divided into four groups. Several of the nicer girls and a couple of the boys who had strict scholastic accountability to professional parents went into her camp almost immediately when they saw that she was systematic, skillful, and just. Another group, whose names and faces are always hard to remember, went along with her because they sensed that she was a stronger personality; that balking would be tiring, involve exposure of weakness, and end in failure. These two groups accounted for perhaps two-thirds of the class. In the remaining third were the Idiot rebels and the Hard-Nut rebels.

The Idiots moved in first, without seeing where they were going. For example:

Idiot: "Do we *have* to put our names on our compositions?" (looking around at the other Idiots for appreciative laughter).

Miss B.: "You don't *have* to."

Idiot (next day after papers had been passed back): "I didn't get my paper back. I have no grade."

Miss B.: "Did you expect one?"

Idiot: "You said we didn't *have* to put our names on them."

Miss B.: "That's right. You don't *have* to walk around with your eyes open, either."

The Idiot sat down, uneasily. That afternoon his name was up with the absentees who had to make up the composition.

The Idiots were beaten from the start. She was indifferent to petty annoyances, and they did not dare try big ones.

The Hard-Nuts, the long-time class heroes, waited more

patiently, seeking their own ground. Their particular dragon in the case of Miss Barracombie was her good sense, which forced an antagonist to assume a role so foolish as to threaten his status among his classmates. This forced the Hard-Nuts to try to operate outside the teaching periods, in the rather limited areas of truancy, ground rules, and personal relationships.

It was difficult to challenge her with truancy because there our parents were solidly on her side, and besides, the occasional absence or trumped-up tardiness of an individual did little to alter the steady civilizing routine. As for opportunities on the school grounds, Miss Barracombie supervised only in her turn, and was by some unexpected quirk more lenient than any of the other teachers, letting us proceed at games considerably rougher than we wished to be playing.

The worst of the Hard-Nuts was Lennie Sopel. He was big and tough and bearded already, very much in the know about engines, baseball statistics, and older women. He had a way of muttering wisecracks half under his breath when girls recited. At first they reached only to people in the surrounding seats. Then one day Lila Crocker went down the aisle, and Lennie said in a loud whisper that shook the room like an east wind.

"Oh, man. I wish I had that swing in my backyard!"

Miss Barracombie stopped listening to a girl at the study table. The girl stopped talking. Lila fled to the waste basket and back to her seat, her face scarlet.

The room became as silent as a tomb in a pyramid.

Miss Barracombie looked at Lennie for a long time, and he locked eyes with her, ready for a showdown.

"What are you thinking about, Lennie?" she asked at last, rather softly for her.

"Nothin'." He could say that one word as though it were the nastiest in the language. "Absolutely nothin'."

"Well, I'm thinking about something," she said, still calm and relaxed. "You come in at three and I'll tell you about it. In the meantime, stand up."

"What for? What'd I do?"

"Stand up, please."

Lennie hesitated. Again it was one of her simple inescapable requests. He slid out into the aisle and stood up.

Miss Barracombie went back to her work with the girl at the table. Lennie started to sit down once, but she gave him a steady eye and he straightened up again. He had to stand by his seat throughout the rest of the afternoon. We kept looking at him, waiting for him to say something; Lennie couldn't seem to think of anything to say.

She kept him after school forty-five minutes every day for six months. He never spoke out of turn again in class and he never missed a session with her. It seemed a heavy punishment for one remark, and we couldn't get over either her giving it or his taking it. When we asked him what he had to do, all he would say was "nothin'."

"For forty hours, Lennie?"

"Who's countin'? And whose business is it?"

Then one day Alice Rowe gave us the lowdown. She had been helping in the inner office when the intercom was open to Miss Barracombie's room.

"She's teaching him to read."

Nobody would believe her. "Lennie's in seventh grade," everybody said. "He knows how to read."

"No, he doesn't," Alice said. "I heard him stumbling over the littlest words up there. Who's ever heard him read in class?"

We tried to remember when we had heard Lennie read. He was a transfer to us in the fourth grade, and there hadn't been much oral reading since then.

"How does he do his other work?" we asked.

"Who says he does?"

No wonder Lennie couldn't fight her. She taught him in secret the one thing he needed to have before giving up cheating and pretending.

The truth was, no rebellion had a chance with her. She wasn't mean and she never struck anybody (although our parents queried us over and over again on this point, wanting, we thought, to be able to say, *Of course she has order! She whips them.*). No situation could come up that she would not know how to handle efficiently and without damage to her single drive: she would teach; we would learn.

Whatever we studied, we mastered. Of course, she knew the ones of us who could not connect with the main lines she was trolling, but she put out other lines for them and they mastered, too. Nobody was free not to learn. We were free to fail, but somehow a failure was not a separate thing, only a step in learning. She never assumed that we had achieved. She probed and exposed until she read it in the blood. A week later when we were not expecting it, she would check again. She was the only teacher whose grades on our report cards we never questioned. Nor would we let our indignant parents go to her. She knew.

This was no love affair between the class and Miss Barracombie, however. She was businesslike and not tender with us. She encouraged no intimacies, and the thought of confiding in her as we had in Miss Tondreau who used to love us in the third grade was wholly ridiculous. We were just different with her. When our special teachers came and Miss Barracombie left the room, Eugene Kent would replace his hearing-aid, and we would be at once on the Plain of Esdraelon[5], stalking a world of enemies. By the end of the period our specials would be limp and distraught.

We did no better left on our own. If Miss Barracombie stepped out of the room—something she wisely did rarely—we would have the ceiling. After all, we had been indulged for years. Thirty near-simians don't slough that off in a few stretching months. We had never been convinced that discipline comes from within, and when the restraining presence was removed we reverted to the barbarians that we were.

Miss Barracombie never mentioned our behavior with other teachers or when she was out of the room, although the specials must have complained bitterly. It seemed to be part of her code that she was responsible when she was left with us and others were responsible when they took us. We liked that. Miss Barracombie did not lecture or make us feel guilty. There was nothing to lecture or feel guilty about. We behaved. We learned. We had to: it was the contract.

But the final lesson we learned from Miss Barracombie was one she did not try to teach us. It was during the last period. We were in the midst of a discussion on the use of quotation marks. The intercom box pinged on the wall and the principal said:

"A telegram has just arrived for you, Miss Barracombie. Will you send a boy down for it?"

She sent Herbert Harvey Bell. He was in the corner seat by the door. He went out running because she knew exactly how long it took to get to the office and back and he did not want to answer for loitering.

[5] *Armageddon*

He returned with the telegram, gave it to her, and took his seat.

She opened the envelope calmly and neatly so as not to tear the inside sheet. Still reading it, she turned about slowly so that her back was toward the class. Her hands lowered. We could see that she was no longer looking at the telegram but at the bulletin board. She did not turn back to us. She kept looking at something on the board.

Then before the alerted, somehow apprehensive eyes of the class, Miss Barracombie began to grow smaller. It was in her shoulders first. They began to narrow, to go forward. Her back curved. Her head dropped. We waited, not knowing what to do. Herbert Harvey Bell seemed to feel the most responsible. He looked around at all of us with a question in his wide, stunned eyes. We had nothing for him. Herbert Harvey Bell pulled himself up from his seat and ran across the hall to the teacher there.

Lennie Sopel had started down from his seat, but when he saw the other teacher, Mrs. Hamilton, coming, he turned and went back up the aisle.

Mrs. Hamilton went up to Miss Barracombie and peered into her face. Then she bent to the telegram still in her hands.

"Oh, my dear," she said, putting her arm around Miss Barracombie. Miss Barracombie did not move. Her shoulders were gone, melted into her narrow back.

Mrs. Hamilton turned her in the direction of the door. Our teacher put both hands across her face and, huddled and small, walked out like a child under Mrs. Hamilton's arm.

No one breathed or moved. A few minutes later Mrs. Hamilton looked into our room.

"Miss Barracombie has lost someone dear to her, boys and girls. Try to finish the period quietly."

No one came near us for the rest of the afternoon, not even to dismiss us. But we did not behave as we usually did when left alone. Most of us took out our composition notebooks and pens. Some just sat there.

We were frightened—a little sad for Miss Barracombie, of course—but mainly frightened, and frightened for ourselves. If *she* could be struck down, who was so tall, so erect, with all things under control, what could not happen to the rest of us who never had any control on the inside, who had to be made by others to hold our shoulders back?

We were the best we had ever been until the bell rang that day. For a moment we could see our connection with adults. Through a maze of equivalent fractions and common denominators we could see other people, huddled and shrinking, being led out of strange rooms. And their faces were ours.

Teresa Feley

Teresa Feley wrote for popular magazines during the second half of the twentieth century.

BOBBIE
SHAFTOE

Author Unknown

This is a hard story for a teacher to read—especially the ending. We give grades in deportment and citizenship, both euphemisms for doing nothing and speaking only when the teacher's green light is on. Yet the undeniable truth is that, more often than not, it will be the mischievous ones, the proverbial pains in the neck, who truly succeed, who go on to blaze new trails.

Bobbie Shaftoe was one of those latter ones—until the sudden storm. . . . I wonder whether the ending is really a happy one. Or is it perhaps tragic?

Bobbie Shaftoe's gone to sea,
Silver buckles on his knee.
He'll come back and marry me.
Pretty Bobbie Shaftoe.

This old and musical nursery rhyme had been ringing in my head all day as I went about my work. My work was teaching a district school halfway between Garret's Mills and Bentley's Dam—so situated in order to accommodate children from both villages.

Why that ancient nursery rhyme should have been singing itself in my head all day, I do not know, unless it was because one of my pupils, popularly known as Bobbie Shaftoe, had, that morning, given me an unusual amount of trouble. How and when he received the nickname, I never heard. Perhaps it was because of his oft-declared ambition to be a sailor and to go to sea; possibly it was because of a similarity of sound between this name and the real one. He was ten years old, bright and active, and the most mischievous child I had ever seen; not maliciously mischievous, but good-naturedly, irrepressibly, unceasingly mischievous. Such mild punishment as his mirthful misdemeanor deserved had but momentary effect on him, and one must have had an unusually hard heart to have chastised Bobbie with any degree of severity.

On the June day of which I write, Bobbie was more than ordinarily full of pranks and practical jokes. He had been busy with them all the bright morning, and he was holding his own steadily through the hot and sultry afternoon. I had reprimanded him, times without number; I had punished him mildly time and again, without lasting effect. Finally I seated him on the top of a cold stove in order to humiliate him, but from that conspicuous perch his comical motions and queer grimaces, when my back was turned, kept the entire school snickering, until I took him down. After that he made an amusing picture on his slate, of himself sitting on the stove, and held it up to be laughed at by the boys in his vicinity; but before I could capture it, his sponge had obliterated forever this triumph of his art. His next achievement that afternoon was the production of little pasteboard figures of men, pinned to a stick, and fighting each other furiously as his deft fingers pulled the string attached to them. I caught him at it squarely.

"Let me have them, Bobbie," said I.

He turned them over to me without a murmur, explaining as he did so, "You pull thith thtring w'en he knockth 'em down. I'll thow you, thee? Don't they jutht lambath each other, though?"

It is needless to say that the school was again diverted; everyone, save Bobbie and me, grinned broadly. He was sober and I was annoyed. "Give them to me at once," I said sharply. "What am I going to do with such a boy? How shall I punish you? I have tried everything except a severe whipping. Shall I give you that? Or can you suggest something else?"

He cast his eyes to the ceiling and screwed up his mouth comically, as if in intense thought. The school broke out in renewed laughter. Finally he said, "You might put me up in the loft, Mith Mitchell. I haven't been up there yet."

"Very well," I replied quickly. "Up into the loft you go."

He was a little staggered at the suddenness of my decision. I don't think he really expected me to adopt his suggestion, for the loft was not a pleasant place to go into. It was dark, hot, and empty, with the roof sloping down on each side, so that only through the middle of it could a boy stand erect.

"Here, Bobbie," I continued, "help me to set this table under the opening—that's it. Now give me that chair."

The horizontal aperture that led to the loft was just over the high platform that stretched across the rear end of the room, and with the aid of a chair placed on the table, one could readily climb up to it.

"You hold fatht to the chair an' don't let her thlip," cautioned Bobbie as he hitched up his suspenders, screwed up his face, and made ready for his grand ascent.

He climbed to the table, mounted the chair, and thrust his head and shoulders through the opening, out of sight. He drew them down again in a moment to say, "It'th dark up there, Mith Mitchell."

"I know it," I replied calmly.

"An' hot."

"I know it."

"An'—an'—lonethome."

"That's why I'm sending you up there."

"Well," he sighed, "here goeth. Good-by."

He reached up, grasped the framework of the opening, and in the next instant he had drawn his pliant little body up out of sight. I lifted the chair down, and removed the table, and tried to go on with the routine of recitations. There was some scrambling above in the loft; once I saw a bare brown foot twinkling down through the opening for a second, for the edification of all of Bobbie's fellow pupils, and once a dust-begrimed face, inverted and comical, looked carefully down and set the school in a new uproar.

"Bobbie," I called out to him finally, "put the cover down on the opening at once." I had not thought to have this done; it would make it so dark up there; but his irrepressible mischief left me no recourse.

"Yeth'm," he replied still cheerfully. "Thall I thit on it to hold it down?"

"Certainly."

The cover, which was on hinges, was carefully let down, and this movement was immediately followed by a thud, which indicated that Bobbie was "thitting on it." After that, save certain indefinable sounds, all was quiet in the region of the loft.

The afternoon tasks went on monotonously. The day grew more sultry as it drew to its close. Just before it was time to dismiss school, one of my pupils, a little girl, after looking out a moment through the open door, into the dusty road, rose quickly from her seat, threw up her hand, and began to snap vigorously with her finger and thumb to attract my attention.

"Well, what is it, Rosie?" I inquired.

"Please, Miss Mitchell, Bobbie Shaftoe is out there in the road."

"Who?" I asked in amazement.

"Bobbie Shaftoe. He's out there hiding behind a tree."

Of course, everyone turned and looked out of the door. At that moment a little figure darted out from the shadow of one tree and sought shelter behind another. It was indeed Bobbie Shaftoe. How he managed to make his escape from the loft I could not conjecture.

I went to the door and called, "Bobbie! Bobbie! Bobbie Shaftoe!"

He left the protection of the tree at once. "Yeth'm," he replied, "I'm coming."

He had evidently hurt his foot in some way, as he limped slightly as he came up the steps.

"Take your seat, Bobbie," I said sternly, "and don't move out of it until I give you permission to do so."

He hung his head a trifle as if he were ashamed at last of his deeds, dropped into his seat, and sat there in perfect quiet during the few minutes that intervened before school closed. I dismissed the pupils somewhat ahead of time, as there seemed a thunder-shower coming in the west, and I wished them to get to their homes before it rained; but Bobbie I kept with me to punish him. I had my monthly report to make out. I had thought of keeping him in his seat during the hour that I should be thus occupied. He sat quietly, but had taken up a book and begun to study.

After a while my curiosity got the better of my determination, and I said to him, "Bobbie, will you tell me how you escaped from the loft?"

He answered, "Yeth'm, I opened the thcuttle hole in the roof—it'th right up there, you know—and I climbed out on the ridgepole; there'th a limb of that big elm hangth right down there, and I got on that and then it was eathy to thlide down to the ground."

The escape shorn of its mystery was simple enough after all. A low ominous roll of thunder ended in a bass so deep and power-ful that it sent a tremor through the building.

"Bobbie," I said with a sudden resolution, "I wish you wouldn't give me so much trouble. I don't want to be scolding and punishing you all the time. I like you too well for that."

Bobbie looked at me with calm seriousness in his deep blue eyes. "I've been thinkin' about that, Mith Mitchell," he replied.

"I like you too. I'm goin' to thtop it. I am goin' to try to be better."

"Oh, will you, Bobbie?"

"I will."

I saw by the quiet look of resolution on his face that he meant it.

"Thank you, Bobbie," I exclaimed, taking both his little brown hands in mine.

I was going to say something else to him, but a sharp flash of lightning, followed in a second by a crack and a crash of thunder, interrupted me. I hastened to shut the doors and close the windows and lower such apologies for shades as we had. Sudden darkness fell upon us, and thunderings were incessant. I sat on the steps of the platform and held Bobbie's hand, thankful for human company and sympathy. The rain came and fell, not in drops, but in sheets and layers. In a minute the public road in front of us was a dashing torrent. In another, the schoolhouse lot was a miniature lake. But the terrible stormbursts soon passed us by. The roar of the rain died away toward the east. After a little while the sky began to brighten, and I gained courage to look from the window on the washed and flooded landscape. Bobbie had behaved like a hero. Not one word had passed from his lips, and beyond the slight pallor of his face, one could see in it no signs of fear.

"I gueth it'th gone by now, Mith Mitchell," he said. "Wathn't it a big one, though?"

The words were scarcely out of his mouth when a new sound came to our ears—a sound more ominous than any we had heard yet, increasing in volume with every passing second. Bobbie stood for a moment intently listening, then dashed to the platform, tore back the shade from the window, and we both looked out.

"It'th Bentley'th Dam," he cried. "It'th butht."

Far up the ravine, where Coulters Creek came dancing through in the summertime, a solid mass of water was sweeping down toward us, crested with the debris of its journey. It would strike the pond, flood the narrow valley, and wash the schoolhouse from its foundation. This was inevitable, yet there was no escape. Before we could cross half the distance to the nearest house the water would be upon us. I started back into the room and covered my face with my hands.

Bobbie stood for a moment in fearful indecision, then he flung his arms toward the ceiling and cried, "The loft—the roof—the tree!"

I grasped the idea at once. In it lay the only hope of safety. We seized the table and placed it in position, flung the chair on it, and the next moment Bobbie was shoving up the cover with herculean strength. It yielded and fell back. He plunged upward into the darkness of the loft, and had his hands down to help me before I had fairly gained the chair. The next moment we were both climbing out at the scuttle to the ridge of the roof. Even as we did so, the flood came down. It was deafening to hear and so frightful to see. On its crest were the wrecks of houses, and in its foam dead bodies were tossed. It struck the pond and then swept on to the dam, the bridge, and then the narrow gorge below us; and then, checked in its progress, came leaping, flooding up the bank, across the road, rising with fearful rapidity to the windows of the schoolhouse, rolling out into the field a boiling, foam-flecked wall of death and destruction.

"Grab it, quick! Go up!" Bobbie was calling, as he held the limb of the tree within my reach.

I was weak from fright and the swirling waters made my head swim. I grasped the limb, and pulled myself along on it, but so slowly and awkwardly that Bobbie, losing his hold, caught my foot and pushed me upward. The water was at the eaves; the schoolhouse was swaying on its foundation.

I caught and clung wildly to the next branch above my head and cried out, "Save yourself, Bobbie! Hurry, save yourself."

The building lurched ponderously to one side as Bobbie grasped for the limb, missed it, and fell back onto the ridgepole of the roof. He caught hold on the framework of the scuttle to save himself from falling into the waves, and clung to it desperately as the building, loosed from its bearings, went sailing out upon the flood. Already the waters were beginning to recede. The schoolhouse, rising and falling, dipping and twisting, went swimming down toward the gorge.

"Good-by," called Bobbie as he went past, "good-by, and hang on tight, Mith Mitchell. I'm goin' to thea."

"Good-by," I called back to him. "O Bobbie, good-by!"

The waves dashed over his head now and again, as he floated out of sight; and even in that dreadful moment, the words of that sweet old nursery rhyme came back to my mind—

> *Bobbie Shaftoe's gone to sea,*
> *Silver buckles on his knee.*
> *He'll come back and marry me.*
> *Pretty Bobbie Shaftoe.*

The flood went down, and the ruined landscape lay bare of water, save in pools and ponds. Twilight descended beautiful as a dream, and through it came the men from the village, seeking the lost and dead, and helped me down from the tree that had saved me. I went shivering to Bobbie Shaftoe's home. At midnight they brought him home. They had found him far down the stream, tangled in the wreckage of the flood. He was not dead, but that was the most hopeful thing one could say of him.

At dawn he flung out his arms from the coverlid. "Hang on tight, Mith Mitchell," he cried weakly. "Good-by, I'm goin' to thea."

"Oh Bobbie," I cried. "Come back to me, brave Bobbie!"

He seemed to hear me, and to understand, for he opened his eyes, and answered, "Yeth, Mith Mitchell, I have been thinkin' about it, an' I will."

And he did. Night and day I sat by him, and nursed him back to health and strength. But when he grew to be well again, his mischievous nature had left him. He was a changed boy. He was sober and studious. And even before the years of his youth had wholly passed, earnest manhood rested on him like a crown.

RESEARCH MAN

W. R. Van Meter

*B*ob downplayed teaching, for research was where the action was. But Polly was seeing weaknesses in her brother she hadn't noticed before. If only something would happen to wake him up.

*T*he room was a big one, flooded with pale-yellow
January sunlight from the bay window that faced the
southwest; but it had obviously never been designed for
its present use. The severely practical aspect of incubators,
chemical glassware, and a much-used autoclave contrasted
strikingly with the gay flowered wall paper and the inviting open
fireplace. These latter gave an impression of a colorful warmth,
unusual in a laboratory.

Polly Rodden, washing culture tubes, looked up expectantly as
her brother hurried in. "Did you get your letter?" she asked
excitedly. "It's from Gates University."

"Here, read it!" Bob thrust the letter toward her eagerly.
"Why, they liked my two research papers in the *Journal* so much
that they're almost begging me to accept a place on their staff!"

Polly glanced at him appraisingly. "They are lucky to get a
research man like you, aren't they?" she murmured, and went on
reading.

Bob grinned at his sister's tone and began quietly to examine
some flasks from the incubator.

Not surprisingly, growing up in a household, the life of which
centered around the demands of a country doctor's profession, it
was inevitable that brother and sister should depend much upon
each other. Since his return from Northwestern University, Bob
had been teaching chemistry at Greenville High School and
working at bacteriological research in his spare time. Polly was a
senior at the high, to graduate in the spring.

"This does sound wonderful, Bob!" Polly said finally.

"Well, of course," he answered, "it's really only an invitation
to come down and interview with them. Still, they must be sold
on me, or they wouldn't go that far. And will I be glad to get out
of teaching at Greenville!"

Polly frowned. "What's the matter with Greenville? Or this lab? Wasn't it here that you did the research for those papers the Gates crowd like?"

Bob put his hands on her shoulders. "Be serious, Polly. You've never seen a real laboratory. Why, down at Gates, every man has a place that is perfect—the most modern lighting and air conditioning, pipes carrying hot and cold water, gas, oxygen, carbon dioxide, and compressed air. I would *work* in a place like that!"

"Maybe," Polly conceded agreeably. "But don't forget that Pasteur had less equipment to help him than you do. Ever hear of the papers he published? And Einstein worked with just a pad of paper and some pencils—plus his mind."

They worked for a while in silence. Then suddenly Polly gave a little gasp of dismay. "Oh, Bob!" she said reproachfully, stabbed by the memory of what she had forgotten. "Nick Brown and Morry Edwards were over here again. They want you to give them special teaching."

"I don't have the time," Bob exclaimed. "I've got to get out another research paper. Why can't they get someone else at the high school to tutor them?"

"There isn't anyone else who knows science the way you do," Polly said flatly. "The boys will be terribly disappointed if—"

Bob shrugged. "Sorry—it's too bad."

Nick Brown and Morry Edwards were seniors at the high school; both of them keen, alert, and with the sharply defined interest in scientific work that invariably precedes a successful career in chemistry. They had come to Bob with the request that he help them prepare for the Grantland examination which every year drew high-school seniors from all over the country to compete for the college scholarships which a wealthy oil man had endowed. Neither the Browns nor the Edwards could afford the expense of four years' technical school training for their sons. Nick and Morry had to have scholarships in order to continue their schooling.

Bob drove the two hundred miles to Philadelphia that weekend for his interview. When he arrived home late, Polly was waiting for him in the living room beside a roaring fire.

"They have a place open," he said exultantly. "Assistant to Joel Laird."

"Why," Polly breathed softly, "he's the most famous bacteriologist in America!" There was a queer mixture of pride and sadness in Polly's eyes as she watched her brother. "Is . . . is everything settled?"

He frowned slightly. "No. Laird has to make the final decision. He had been called to Pittsburgh unexpectedly; so I didn't see him."

Bob finished the last crumbs of the freshly made gingerbread that old Harriet had brought in. Polly stared thoughtfully into the fire.

"From now on," Bob said at last, "every minute I can get goes into research."

He was in the laboratory one afternoon a few days later. Polly helped him make counts on the neat stacks of plates before the incubator.

Old Harriet, panting from the exertion of climbing the stairs, pushed open the laboratory door. "They's a gentleman waiting to see you in the living room, Mr. Bob," she announced. "No one I know, neither. And those two high-school scholars want to speak to you, too."

Polly looked at her brother beseechingly. "Why can't you help them, Bob?"

He was annoyed. "You know why, Polly."

At the foot of the stairs, beside the entrance to the living room, Bob found Nick and Morry waiting anxiously. "Hello," Bob said crisply. "If it's about that teaching for the Grantland exams, I can't give you any time, fellows. Sorry."

Nick Brown looked downcast. "We knew you were busy, Mr. Rodden."

His companion, dark-eyed Morry, interrupted. "And we do need—"

Bob shook his head. "I'm a research man, Morry."

Morry said curtly, "Come on, Nick, let's go!"

Bob watched them for a second as they went down the porch steps; then he entered the living room. "Why, you're Dr. Laird!" he exclaimed, catching sight of his visitor. "I've seen your picture in the *Journal.*"

The older man smiled. He was, Bob saw, broad-shouldered and stocky, and his sharp blue eyes seemed to take in everything at a glance. "I was driving through," he explained, "returning to the university. Since I failed to meet you at Gates, I thought it would be interesting to drop in."

Dr. Laird stayed for dinner that evening. Later that night, when he had driven away, Bob came jubilantly into the living room.

"Did you see how impressed he was?" he asked Polly.

"I heard him say," Polly replied, "that you have a remarkable flair for research work. Sounds promising."

A week went by without any word from Philadelphia. Bob did not realize how anxiously he had been awaiting the letter until it finally came on the tenth day. He tore it open eagerly, while Polly stood beside him, breathless.

"I guess," Bob said tonelessly an instant later, "that settles that!"

"But what do they say?" Polly demanded nervously. "Why do you look so queer, Bob?" She took the paper from his hand and read quickly the few paragraphs. The university had decided to reject his application for a place on their staff. They did not wish him to feel that this was a reflection upon his ability in his field; the university, instead, sought a man of somewhat different talents. The signature to the letter, Polly saw, was that of Joel Laird.

"This Saturday," Bob declared grimly, "I'm going down to Philadelphia and find out what the man means!"

Bob came back from Gates University baffled and uncertain, as one may be on finding that what is unimportant to him is of tremendous significance to others.

"What happened?" Polly asked.

"Nothing," Bob said wearily. "Dr. Laird was very pleasant, but I couldn't make him change his decision."

"What reason did he give?"

Bob sank into a chair. "He said that it was a good thing to be able to do research—"

"What did he mean, then?" Polly asked, puzzled.

Bob continued, "but that being able to teach so that others understand you and are inspired by you was a much greater ability."

Polly, watching him carefully, saw that he had been hurt more than he would ever show.

❧

For two days after this trip, Bob spent all his free time on his research problem, working doggedly. Then, on the third day, he did not go into the laboratory. It was the beginning of a long period during which the door of that room was opened only by Polly.

He spent whole afternoons tramping and skiing through the woods, cold and silent under the snows of winter.

Polly said once, at a Saturday morning breakfast, "Why don't we do some experimental work this afternoon? It's been ages—"

"No. The research won't amount to anything, anyway. I'm going to take a ski run down Nittany to Stony Creek."

Bob shot down the last long slope of Nittany in a burst of speed, turned; and as he slid forward on the level, losing momentum, he came upon Nick and Morry. They were sitting on a log, their skis beside them. Morry was carefully nursing a tiny, fitfully burning fire of damp wood.

Nick looked up. "'Lo," he said. "Feel like a sandwich? We've got some extras."

Bob grinned. He was hungry. "Glad to, Nick." Rid of his skis, he sat down on the log. "What are you doing out here, Nick?" he asked curiously.

Morry, glancing at him sidewise, answered. "We're studying for the Grantland exams."

"Sure," Nick explained. "We work with the books a couple of hours, then quiz each other on the stuff we've been reading all the while we're tramping around. It's a system Morry thought up."

"Oh," Bob said, remembering uncomfortably that he had refused to help them.

"We were having an argument just now," Morry added, "about the periodic table. What good is it—practically, I mean?"

"Lots of good," Nick replied hotly. "You can predict what new elements, that haven't even been discovered, will be like."

Morry openly scorned such use. "Where's the value of that, Nick?"

Quietly Bob interrupted. "Did you ever hear," he asked, "of a man named Midgley, the man who developed the ethyl fluid we use in gasoline today?" He told them, then, the story of how the periodic system of the elements had proved such a perfect research tool for the very practical job of finding a better fuel for high-compression gasoline engines. They talked of chemistry all the way home, and Bob knew a feeling of release which he had not felt for weeks.

"How about going out again, Monday?" Nick asked, as they stood at the Rodden gate.

Bob nodded. "Be glad to."

Afterward, when they had gone, he acknowledged frankly that he was grateful for the invitation. He had not expected a second chance, knowing the keenness of their pride and remembering how ungraciously he had refused them before.

He gave them what he could that second afternoon. They made a date for the next day. It seemed odd to Bob when he noticed that teaching Nick and Morry was having an effect on his general teaching. For a year he had been giving the classes which he taught just about what he was forced to give them. The energy required to do more than this minimum had gone into his research work. How fair had he been? There was more to teaching than just handing out barren facts, the skeleton-like data of science that could be found in any textbook. Now he was trying to stir his classes with the words, thoughts, and deeds of many other men in science. The response which he got in the days that followed thrilled Bob as nothing had done since his first publication in the *Journal*. Meantime Nick and Morry made rapid progress.

Winter slipped imperceptibly into spring until, suddenly, it was late March, and the slopes of Nittany showed widening splotches of soft green where the snow was gone. The examination was to be held during the Easter vacation.

Bob saw Nick and Morry off on the train to New York. The hours dragged. He thought once that it would have been less nerve-racking had he also gone. No, all that he could do was already finished. He had brought them through the preliminary examinations successfully. They had qualified for the finals. In New York, Bob knew, he would be in the way.

Polly brought him the evening papers. There were pictures on the front page of the contestants, gathered in a circle on the lawn of the Grantland, Long Island, estate. Bob gazed for a long while at the blurred newspaper cut—dark-eyed Morry and stubborn, courageous Nick looking out seriously from the page. "Good luck!" he murmured.

They came back on the last train two nights later. Bob and Polly met them at the station.

"How was it?" Polly asked. "Hard?"

Morry gave her his warm smile. "And then some! Wait till you hear some of the questions they asked!"

"Say," Nick demanded, "you know who one of the judges was, Mr. Rodden? He said he knew you. Dr. Laird. We told him about the way you helped us get ready for the exam, and he asked to be remembered to you."

Bob nodded, his mouth a little awry. He had seen Dr. Laird's name among the list of judges. "When are the results made public?" he asked his young pupils.

Morry answered, "We'll hear within a week."

❧

Polly raced in with the paper. "Bob! Bob!" she called excitedly. "They got them. Nick and Morry both got scholarships!"

Bob swung round from the telephone. "Morry just called," he said happily. "Wants us to come over to dinner. Isn't it swell?"

There was a ringing at the front door. They heard Harriet answer it. Then she came into the room, waving a yellow envelope in front of her. "Telegraph for you, Mr. Bob! Wonder what it could be about?"

"Well, wait a minute, and we'll find out," said Polly.

Bob tore it open. He whistled incredulously. "Read it!" he gasped to Polly.

She scanned the slip. "Showing of Brown and Edwards in Grantland exams convinces me you have developed into a teacher. You belong down here at Gates. Can you come at end of present term? Joel Laird."

W. R. Van Meter

W. R. Van Meter wrote for inspirational magazines during the first half of the twentieth century.

THREE LETTERS
FROM TEDDY

Elizabeth Silance Ballard

*T*eachers are supposed to treat every pupil the same. But try as they may, inevitably they favor some and shortchange others.

Teddy she disliked from the very first day. And he knew it. By midyear she was determined to flunk him.

*T*eddy's letter came today, and now that I've read it, I will place it in my cedar chest with the other things that are important to my life.

"I wanted you to be the first to know."

I smiled as I read the words he had written and my heart swelled with a pride that I had no right to feel.

I have not seen Teddy Stallard since he was a student in my fifth grade class, fifteen years ago. It was early in my career, and I had only been teaching for two years.

From the first day he stepped into my classroom, I disliked Teddy. Teachers (although everyone knows differently) are not supposed to have favorites in a class, but most especially they are not to show dislike for a child, *any* child.

Nevertheless, every year there are one or two children that one cannot help but be attached to, for teachers are human, and it is human nature to like bright, pretty, intelligent people, whether they are ten years old or twenty-five. And sometimes (not too often, fortunately), there will be one or two students to whom the teacher can't seem to relate.

I had thought myself quite capable of handling my personal feelings along that line until Teddy walked into my life. There wasn't a child I particularly liked that year, but Teddy was most assuredly one I disliked.

He was dirty. Not just occasionally, but all the time. His hair hung low over his ears, and he actually had to hold it out of his eyes as he wrote his papers in class. (And this was before it was fashionable to do so!) Too, he had a peculiar odor about him which I could never identify.

His physical faults were many, and his intellect left a lot to be desired, as well. By the end of the first week I knew he was hopelessly behind the others. Not only was he behind, he was just plain slow! I began to withdraw from him immediately.

Any teacher will tell you that it's more of a pleasure to teach a bright child. It is definitely more rewarding for one's ego. But any teacher worth her credentials can channel work to the bright child, keeping him challenged and learning while she puts her major efforts on the slower ones. Any teacher *can* do this. Most teachers do it, but I didn't, not that year.

In fact, I concentrated on my best students and let the others follow along as best they could. Ashamed as I am to admit it, I took perverse pleasure in using my red pen; and each time I came to Teddy's papers, the cross marks (and they were many) were always a little larger and a little redder than necessary.

While I did not actually ridicule the boy, my attitude was obviously quite apparent to the class, for he quickly became the class "goat," the outcast, the unlovable and the unloved.

He knew I didn't like him, but he didn't know why. Nor did I know—then or now—why I felt such an intense dislike for him. All I know is that he was a little boy no one cared about, and I made no effort on his behalf.

The days rolled by. We made it through the Fall Festival and the Thanksgiving holidays, and I continued marking happily with my red pen.

As the Christmas holidays approached, I knew that Teddy would never catch up in time to be promoted to the sixth grade level. He would be a repeater.

To justify myself, I went to his cumulative folder from time to time. He had very low grades for the first four years, but no grade failure. How he had made it, I didn't know. I closed my mind to the personal remarks:

First grade: Teddy shows promise by work and attitude, but has poor home situation.

Second grade: Teddy could do better. Mother terminally ill. He receives little help at home.

Third grade: Teddy is a pleasant boy. Helpful, but too serious. Slow learner. Mother passed away end of the year.

Fourth grade: Very slow, but well behaved. Father shows no interest.

Well, they passed him four times, but he will certainly repeat fifth grade! Do him good! I said to myself.

And then the last day before the holiday arrived. Our little tree on the reading table sported paper and popcorn chains. Many gifts were heaped underneath, waiting for the big moment.

Teachers always get several gifts at Christmas, but mine that year seemed bigger and more elaborate than ever. There was not a student who had not brought me one. Each unwrapping brought squeals of delight, and the proud giver would receive effusive thank-yous.

Teddy's gift wasn't the last one I picked up; in fact it was in the middle of the pile. Its wrapping was a brown bag and he had colored Christmas trees and red balls all over it. It was stuck together with masking tape.

"For Miss Thompson—From Teddy" it read.

The group was completely silent, and for the first time I felt conspicuous, embarrassed because they all stood watching me unwrap that gift.

As I removed the last bit of masking tape, two items fell to my desk: a gaudy rhinestone bracelet with several stones missing and a small bottle of dime-store cologne—half empty.

"Isn't this lovely?" I asked, placing the bracelet on my wrist. "Teddy, would you help me fasten it?"

He smiled shyly as he fixed the clasp, and I held up my wrist for all of them to admire.

There were a few hesitant *oohs* and *ahhs*, but as I dabbed the cologne behind my ears, all the little girls lined up for a dab behind their ears.

I continued to open the gifts until I reached the bottom of the pile. We ate our refreshments, and the bell rang.

The children filed out with shouts of "See you next year!" and "Merry Christmas!" but Teddy waited at his desk.

When they had all left, he walked toward me, clutching his gift and books to his chest.

"You smell just like Mom," he said softly. "Her bracelet looks real pretty on you, too. I'm glad you liked it."

He left quickly. I locked the door, sat down at my desk, and wept, resolving to make up to Teddy what I had deliberately deprived him of—a teacher who cared.

I stayed every afternoon with Teddy from the end of the Christmas holidays until the last day of school. Sometimes we worked together. Sometimes we worked alone while I drew up lesson plans or graded papers.

Slowly but surely he caught up with the rest of the class. Gradually there was a definite upward curve in his grades.

He did not have to repeat fifth grade. In fact, his final averages were among the highest in the class, and although I knew he would be moving out of the state when school was out, I was not worried for him. Teddy had reached a level that would stand him in good stead the following year, no matter where he went. He

had enjoyed a measure of success, and as we were taught in our
teacher training course, "success builds success."

I did not hear from Teddy until seven years later, when his first
letter appeared in my mailbox.

> *Dear Miss Thompson,*
> *I just wanted you to be the first to know. I will be graduating*
> *second in my class next month.*
>
> *Very truly yours,*
> *Teddy Stallard*

Four years later, Teddy's second letter came.

> *Dear Miss Thompson,*
> *I wanted you to be the first to know. I was just informed that*
> *I'll be graduating first in my class. The university has not been*
> *easy, but I liked it.*
>
> *Very truly yours,*
> *Teddy Stallard*

I sent him a good pair of sterling silver monogrammed cuff
links and a card, so proud of him I could burst!

❧

And now today—Teddy's third letter.

> *Dear Miss Thompson,*
> *I wanted you to be the first to know. As of today I am Theodore J. Stallard, M.D. How about that!!??*
> *I'm going to be married in July, the 27th, to be exact. I wanted to ask if you could come and sit where my mom would sit if she were here. I'll have no family there as Dad died last year.*
>
> *Very truly yours,*
> *Ted Stallard*

I'm not sure what kind of gift one sends to a doctor on completion of medical school and state boards. Maybe I'll just wait and take a wedding gift, but my note can't wait.

> *Dear Ted,*
> *Congratulations! You made it, and you did it yourself! In spite of those like me and not because of us, this day has come for you. God bless you. I'll be at that wedding with bells on!*

Elizabeth Silance Ballard

Elizabeth Silance Ballard wrote during the second half of the twentieth century.

THE STRANGER WHO
TAUGHT MAGIC

Arthur Gordon

A teacher can also make a real difference outside
the classroom—even during his final moments of life.
Such moments changed the course of a thirteen-year-old
boy's life.

*T*hat July morning, I remember, was like any other—calm and opalescent before the heat of the fierce Georgia sun. I was thirteen, sunburned, shaggy-haired, a little aloof, and solitary. In winter I had to put on shoes and go to school like everyone else. But summers I lived by the sea, and my mind was empty and wild and free.

On this particular morning, I had tied my rowboat to the pilings of an old dock upriver from our village. There, sometimes, the striped sheepshead lurked in the still, green water. I was crouched, motionless as a stone, when a voice spoke suddenly above my head: "Canst thou draw out leviathan with an hook? or his tongue with a cord which thou lettest down?"

I looked up, startled, into a lean pale face and a pair of the most remarkable eyes I had ever seen. It wasn't a question of color; I'm not sure, now, what color they were. It was a combination of things: warmth, humor, interest, alertness. *Intensity*—that's the word, I guess—and, underlying it all, a curious kind of mocking sadness. I believe I thought him old.

He saw how taken aback I was. "Sorry," he said. "It's a bit early in the morning for the book of Job, isn't it?" He nodded at the two or three fish in the boat. "Think you could teach me how to catch those?"

Ordinarily, I was wary of strangers, but anyone interested in fishing was hardly a stranger. I nodded, and he climbed down into the boat. "Perhaps we should introduce ourselves," he said. "But then again, perhaps not. You're a boy willing to teach, I'm a teacher willing to learn. That's introduction enough. I'll call you *Boy,* and you call me *Sir.*"

Such talk sounded strange in my world of sun and salt water. But there was something so magnetic about the man, and so disarming about his smile, that I didn't care.

I gave him a hand line and showed him how to bait his hooks with fiddler crabs. He kept losing baits because he could not recognize a sheepshead's stealthy tug, but he seemed content not to catch anything. He told me he had rented one of the weathered bungalows behind the dock. "I needed to hide for a while," he said. "Not from the police, or anything like that. Just from friends and relatives. So don't tell anyone you've found me, will you?"

I was tempted to ask where he was from; there was a crispness in the way he spoke that was very different from the soft accents I was accustomed to. But I didn't. He had said he was a teacher, though, and so I asked what he taught.

"In the school catalog they call it English," he said. "But I like to think of it as a course in magic—in the mystery and magic of words. Are you fond of words?"

I said that I had never thought much about them. I also pointed out that the tide was ebbing, that the current was too strong for more fishing, and that in any case it was time for breakfast.

"Of course," he said, pulling in his line. "I'm a little forgetful about such things these days." He eased himself back onto the dock with a little grimace, as if the effort cost him something. "Will you be back on the river later?"

I said that I would probably go casting for shrimp at low tide.

"Stop by," he said. "We'll talk about words for a while, and then perhaps you can show me how to catch shrimp."

So began a most unlikely friendship, because I did go back. To this day, I'm not sure why. Perhaps it was because, for the first time, I had met an adult on terms that were in balance. In the realm of words and ideas, he might be the teacher. But in my own small universe of winds and tides and sea creatures, the wisdom belonged to me.

Almost every day after that, we'd go wherever the sea gods or my whim decreed. Sometimes up the silver creeks, where the terrapin skittered down the banks and the great blue herons stood like statues. Sometimes along the ocean dunes, fringed with graceful sea oats, where by night the great sea turtles crawled and by day the wild goats browsed. I showed him where the mullet swirled and where the flounder lay in cunning camouflage. I learned that he was incapable of much exertion; even pulling up the anchor seemed to exhaust him. But he never complained. And, all the time, talk flowed from him like a river.

Much of it I have forgotten now, but some comes back as clear and distinct as if it all happened yesterday, not decades ago. We might be sitting in a hollow of the dunes, watching the sun go down in a smear of crimson. "Words," he'd say. "Just little black marks on paper. Just sounds in the empty air. But think of the power they have! They can make you laugh or cry, love or hate, fight or run away. They can heal or hurt. They even come to look and sound like what they mean. Angry looks angry on the page. Ugly sounds ugly when you say it. Here!" He would hand me a piece of shell. "Write a word that looks or sounds like what it means."

I would stare helplessly at the sand.

"Oh," he'd cry, "you're being dense. There are so many! Like *whisper . . . leaden . . . twilight . . . chime.* Tell you what: When you go to bed tonight, think of five words that look like what they mean and five that sound like what they mean. Don't go to sleep until you do!"

And I would try—but always fall asleep.

Or we might be anchored just offshore, casting into the surf for sea bass, our little bateau nosing over the rollers like a restless hound. "Rhythm," he would say. "Life is full of it; words should have it, too. But you have to train your ear. Listen to the waves on a quiet night; you'll pick up the cadence. Look at the patterns the wind makes in dry sand and you'll see how syllables in a sentence should fall. Do you know what I mean?"

My conscious self didn't know; but perhaps something deep inside me did. In any case, I listened.

I listened, too, when he read from the books he sometimes brought: Kipling, Conan Doyle, Tennyson's *Idylls of the King.* Often he would stop and repeat a phrase or a line that pleased him. One day, in Malory's *Le Morte d'Arthur,* he found one: "And the great horse grimly neighed." "Close your eyes," he said to me, "and say that slowly, out loud." I did. "How did it make you feel?"

"It gives me the shivers," I said truthfully. He was delighted.

But the magic that he taught was not confined to words; he had a way of generating in me an excitement about things I had always taken for granted. He might point to a bank of clouds. "What do you see there? Colors? That's not enough. Look for towers and draw-bridges. Look for dragons and griffins and strange and wonderful beasts."

Or he might pick up an angry claw-brandishing blue crab, holding it cautiously by the back flippers as I had taught him. "Pretend you're this crab," he'd say. "What do you see through those stalklike eyes? What do you feel with those complicated legs? What goes on in your tiny brain? Try it for just five seconds. Stop being a boy. Be a crab!" And I would stare in amazement at the furious creature, feeling my comfortable identity lurch and sway under the impact of the idea. So the days went by. Our excursions became less frequent, because he tired so easily. He brought two chairs down to the dock and some books, but he didn't read much. He seemed content to watch me as I fished, or the circling gulls, or the slow river coiling past.

A sudden shadow fell across my life when my parents told me I was going to camp for two weeks. On the dock that afternoon I asked my friend if he would be there when I got back. "I hope so," he said gently.

But he wasn't. I remember standing on the sun-warmed planking of the old dock, staring at the shuttered bungalow and feeling a hollow sense of finality and loss. I ran to Jackson's grocery store—where everyone knew everything—and asked where the schoolteacher had gone.

"He was sick, real sick," Mrs. Jackson replied. "Doc phoned his relatives up north to come get him. He left something for you—he figured you'd be asking for him."

She handed me a book. It was a slender volume of verse, *Flame and Shadow,* by someone I had never heard of: Sara Teasdale. The corner of one page was turned down, and there was a penciled star by one of the poems. I still have the book, with the poem "On the Dunes."

> *If there is any life when death is over,*
> *These tawny beaches will know much of me,*
> *I shall come back, as constant and as changeful*
> *As the unchanging, many-colored sea.*
> *If life was small, if it has made me scornful,*
> *Forgive me; I shall straighten like a flame*
> *In the great calm of death, and if you want me*
> *Stand on the sea-ward dunes and call my name.*

Well, I have never stood on the dunes and called his name. For one thing, I never knew it; for another, I'd be too self-conscious.

And there are long stretches when I forget all about him. But sometimes—when the music or the magic in a phrase makes my skin tingle, or when I pick up an angry blue crab, or when I see a dragon in the flaming sky—sometimes I remember.

Arthur Gordon
(1912–2002)

During his long and memorable career, Arthur Gordon edited such magazines as *Cosmopolitan, Good Housekeeping,* and *Guideposts.* He was the author of a number of books, including *Reprisal* (1950), *Norman Vincent Peale: Minister to Millions* (1958), *A Touch of Wonder* (1983), and *Return to Wonder* (1996), as well as several hundred short stories.

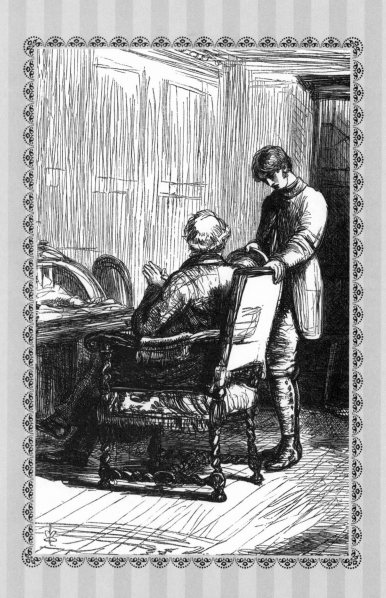

I CAN SEE HIM

Joseph Leininger Wheeler

It always seemed to take forever—that slow walk from parking lot to office, or office to classroom. During the bad times, it would take even longer. During the worst times, he would not come in at all—only his voice would show up (in recordings) to speak to his classes. But the voice, divorced from the body language and slightly sardonic eyes, was a most inadequate substitute.

S trange, how clear it remains in my all-too-often fuzzy memory, forty-some years later. I may not be able to remember where I put my checkbook or a name I have known all my life, but the image and personality of this history professor remain as clear to me as what I see, hear, and experience today.

Like most college students, I was struggling for bedrock between two worlds: the world of my family and childhood and that rather frightening world of adulthood and responsibility. I was shy and insecure, doubting whatever gifts the Creator had entrusted to me. Oh, that was not my façade, which could veer between the brash and the naïve, but that *was* the boy/man cowering behind that inconsistent front. My first role models, my parents, had completed (for better or worse) their job. Unbeknownst to me, I was now searching for a new guiding light, friend, inspiration, mentor, hero. I found all of these in Dr. Walter Utt those many years ago.

It is said, *Show me your mentors, and I'll show you who you will someday be.* I agree, in part. I say "in part" because mentoring that churns out mere clones is not real mentoring; *real* mentors are prospectors seeking to find gold within the vast accumulations of shale each of us houses within. Not transplanted gold, for that is mere watering of the mine, but the gold God buries somewhere in the strata of each child born on this planet. I point this out because all too often our mentors disregard the gold mine within us and sell us instead a bill of goods. Adulation is, after all, the headiest of wines, and rare is the man or woman who can steel the heart and mind against it. To switch metaphors: the natural tendency is for the mentor to fill the empty bottle of the mentoree with self, to create a clone. I have seen those mentored, years later, belatedly wake up to the sad realization that everything they felt was their own was in reality someone else's—their inner gold remained unsearched for and undiscovered. And they then hate that long-ago mentor for raping selfhood.

Were Dr. Utt that kind of mentor, I would not be bringing him back this warm spring day so many years later. He was as different as . . . well . . . as his lectures. And to really explain those, I'll need to take you time traveling—back to the 1950s.

I came to Pacific Union College in California's famed Napa Valley because—well, because my father had gone there and because his parents still lived nearby. Like most missionary kids, I came back to America out of sync. Socially and in sports I was an utter misfit. My sense of self-worth continued to erode. So did my up-till-then high grades. Failure—utter and complete failure—stared me in the face. And I hadn't the slightest inkling of how I could stave off disaster.

Enter Dr. Utt.

Oh, to be honest, I did have other mentors too—notably Professors Lewis Hartin and Paul Quimby—none of us has but one mentor. But, powerful as each of them was, compared to the gravitational drawing power of Dr. Utt's magnetic field, it was no contest.

Looking back at those rootless years, I ricocheted like a drunken bee, trying everything, sipping countless nectars, floundering ever deeper into the morass of failure. I started out in theology because I came from a long line of ministers. But I felt no personal commitment to that calling. Greek came early in my curriculum, and my lackadaisical study habits doomed me to failure there, where getting behind just one class greased your downward skid. Procrastination in Greek is inevitably fatal.

In my freshman year, the college unleashed upon its students a wild experiment: a two-year introduction to the world of

ideas—literature, art, history, music, science, sociology, psychology, philosophy, and religion. Dr. Utt was one of the program's
guiding gurus, and he team-taught the humanities courses. I
listened to him and was fascinated. He and the program opened
up a door into a world I barely knew existed.

Some time later, I finally gathered together my shreds of courage and signed up for one of Dr. Utt's history classes. It was all
that I had heard it would be—and more. Later on I discovered
that Dr. Utt never used the same set of notes twice. As chair of
the history department, student advisor, and campus patron saint
(term used advisedly), he was *always* surrounded by students—
figuratively and sometimes literally sitting at his feet—listening
and asking questions, a number content just to be near him and
to bask in his presence. Perhaps because of his fragility (he was a
hemophiliac and bled easily), we valued his wisdom all the more.
Somehow, in the midst of all these interruptions, he managed to
sketch out his class lecture in his inimitable hieroglyphics on
whatever small piece of paper—often an envelope—was in range.
By the time he painfully pushed out of the chair with the aid of
his ever-present cane, he'd be ready for that next class.

We'd hear the shuffle of his shoes and the tap of his cane long
before we'd see him. There in his classroom we'd be chuckling
over the latest cartoons, usually from the *Saturday Evening Post*.
His favorites had to do with world politics and history. But when
he finally approached the desk, we'd open our tablets, grab a pen,
and look up with an air of expectancy. Fools that we were, each
time we'd vow that *this time,* it would be different. And each
time it would be the same. Before very many moments had
passed, we'd have lost all track of contemporary life and be
immersed in another time. The past, to him, was always a story—
the story of unforgettable people. Those worlds became reality as

Dr. Utt peopled them with flesh and blood. Words he wielded with all the finesse of a knight wielding a rapier made of Toledo tempered steel. Profundities were camouflaged with wit and understatement; one moment, we'd be vainly trying to hold back tears, and another we'd be rolling in the aisles. (His wit was wicked.)

Looking back at it, his stories seem akin to the unvarnished biographies in Scripture, complete with all the frailties, the full range of human thought and behavior. We felt we *knew* Utt's men and women; even in their mistakes of judgment, their trage-dies, we *understood* why they acted as they did. And we felt part of the fabric of the age itself; given the stage upon which they lived, most likely we'd have been hard put to do much better, be much wiser, than they, had we been in their places. Out of all this came Dr. Utt's supreme gift to us—tolerance.

Often we'd feel set up. Funniest, in retrospect, is to remember those who belatedly realized, all at once, a multi-tiered joke (complete with double, triple, and even quadruple entendres), and who convulsively rocked in a vain effort to bottle it up inside. Most often, they'd fail. In the uproar that ensued we'd sometimes catch the sardonic grin: *All that work not wasted after all—someone had caught it!*

Through it all, we never for a moment doubted Utt's basic empathy with the players he brought back to life. Or that, no matter the hells set loose by the Dark Power, God remained at the helm. A kind, loving, forgiving, empathetic God—He alone being capable of separating motive from act.

Then the bell would ring, the mists of another time would dissolve, the images blur, and contemporary time resume. We'd ruefully glance down at page after page of feverishly scrawled notes and know for a certainty that nothing after all was different;

our words could not possibly recapture that magic of *being there* in the past. We'd compare notes and discover that even verbatim transcripts were lifeless without the visual reality of Dr. Utt's presence. It was a compensatory gift from God, one of a kind. I've tried—oh, how I've tried! —to do the same, but I've failed every time. It was his gift alone. No other individual I have ever known has had the power to transport one into a three-dimensional Technicolor past, using mere words.

Those were halcyon days in the college on the hill. Parochial colleges are, after all, subject to the same ebb and flow, the same ideological pendulum swings, experienced by society at large. It was then the twilight of Norman Rockwell America: Family and Judeo-Christian values were still paramount. Because of that societal serenity, liberals, centrists, and conservatives lived at peace with each other on our campus. There was almost perfect balance—I have never seen the like since.

Powerful professors sparked our imaginations and provided a vision for what we might someday become. The greatest Christian thinkers have invariably been well educated: Moses, Daniel, Paul, Augustine, and Luther, to name just a few. For such titans, faith and intellect have blended seamlessly. From each of my professors, I learned and I grew. Some were pure otherworldly intellects; some were grandstanding prima donnas; some were solid centrists; some were mavericks; some were Dostoyevskian Ivans (challenging everything); some were rockbound conservatives, preaching the true faith, and that only. And some, a precious Gideon's band, were Christian Renaissance men and women, embracing the entire philosophical spectrum. The chief of these was Dr. Utt.

On Sabbaths we'd throng the rooms where the Great Ones—various learned professors—held forth. There was always a core lesson for a base, but it represented merely an ideological hockey puck; it might go *anywhere* once the invocation had been given. How their minds sizzled! How they delighted in doing spiritual and intellectual battle with each other! We students rarely dared to enter the lists; we'd have been pulverized in seconds. But we listened—oh, how we listened! And, as we listened, as we assimilated, as we decided whom we agreed with and whom we disagreed with . . . we *grew*. And Dr. Utt was always, health permitting, in the center of the fray. By the twinkle in his eyes, we sensed his inner joy.

On Saturday evenings Dr. Elmer Herr, another history professor, brought the world to our door in his Lyceum Series. It might be a symphony orchestra, it might be Arthur Rubinstein, it might be Fred Waring and his choir, it might be a drama, it might be a film. The best and the finest came to Irwin Hall, and it was unthinkable not to be there with your date.

Each history class I took from Dr. Utt did something to me, strengthened me. Eventually, I changed my major to history. I got Dr. Utt to take me on as his reader, a role I cherished for three years, the last one as graduate assistant.

I can see him now, in that long history office. Every once in a while I'd look up in response to his chuckle, as a particular *Saturday Evening Post* cartoon tickled his funny bone. His other obsessions, such as stamp collecting (especially from France and Monaco), military uniform prints, and anything having to do with the Reformation (especially Huguenots and Waldenses), gave zest to his days. And always there were my obnoxious classmates butting in and taking Dr. Utt's precious time. I was jealous, for I wanted all of him for myself. Some of these ever-present devotees at least expressed themselves intelligently, but there were others who gushed, fawned, and bored me and my fellow readers to death. What they said was so incredibly inane and naïve. Surely Dr. Utt would put them in their place and tell them how monumentally stupid they were. But he *never* did. Never once during those years do I remember him in any way putting them down or lowering their feelings of self-worth. *He was invariably kind.* That was especially impressive to me as I had seen how thoroughly he could dispatch peer opponents in debate (no quarters were given in that arena).

In retrospect, I can see how much like Christ's disciples we were—attempting to drive out the children in order to have the teacher all to ourselves. Also, while in retrospect I can now see Dr. Utt clearly, at that time I most definitely could not. Funny, isn't it, how the Creator programs us to flower gradually? Emily Dickinson put it this way:

> *The Truth must dazzle gradually*
> *Or every man be blind—*

Well, the years passed by, and eventually I took every class, undergraduate and graduate, Dr. Utt offered. Married then, I left to build on my own dreams. But it didn't take long for me to realize how tough the real world was. My first year's teaching came close to being my last. During that traumatic period, when it seemed my only logical alternative was to resign, my wife and I agonized and were never far from tears. Was this the end?

I'll never forget that early spring day. We got in our car and, seemingly on its own volition, it took us west, west to the Napa Valley, then north to Angwin and the home of my mentor. We walked into an Utt family reunion, but they all welcomed us in. Almost instantly Dr. Utt read our faces: "Out with it, Joe. What's wrong?" I told him, and them. Late that afternoon we left, with

stiffer backbones than we'd arrived with earlier, and the Utt
injunction *Fight it out!* ringing in our heads all the way home. We
did—and won. I stayed in teaching.

The telephone rang in my office in Thousand Oaks, California,
twenty-four years later. I picked up the receiver and brightened
momentarily—it was an old college friend. But I quickly sobered
with his next words: "Joe, Dr. Utt just died!"

A part of me died that day.

Then my friend provided details. Dr. Utt had fallen and
needed an immediate blood transfusion. In those days there were
not the controls that there are today, and consequently the blood
he received was contaminated with the AIDS virus. In Dr. Utt's
weakened state, the end came quickly. There was to be a remem-
brance service that coming weekend. Could I be there?

All during the trip north, I thought about Dr. Utt and his role
in whatever I had been able to accomplish in life. I thought back
to those years on campus when he had served as my bridge
between adolescence and adulthood. But I thought even more
about the years afterwards, how he had somehow found time in
his hectic schedule to stay in touch. His notes were like all else
that he laboriously scrawled: brief, pithy, cryptic, funny, and
Utt-ish. As the darker days of the sixties and seventies had
replaced the serene fifties, he'd sometimes note that the ideological climate had changed—"The brethren are at it again"—and I'd
decode it to read: *Some of the ultraconservatives perceive me as a
liberal, and they are making it rather tough for me.* That was as close as
he ever came to complaining. But since he always understated his
problems, I knew by such an admission that things hadn't been

easy for him in recent months. As for his physical ailments, not once did I ever hear him complain!

Those infrequent but cherished cards or short letters never failed to bring a smile.

After bemoaning having to sell his general stamp collection in order to do research in Europe, he ruefully noted:

> *I am trying to force myself to ignore stamps and stick to my writing projects. . . . It's a quiet year, 1,400 students. Few very vocal. Agitation goes in cycles, I think. Faculty is sort of different too. I keep busy, 100 majors. . . . Regards to the Gracious Stabilizer of the Wheeler household.*
> —Card of November 22, 1965

On hearing of our moving east to teach in an Alabama college, he wrote:

> *Happy to hear the news. I hope that this will prove a rewarding experience. I don't think there's any doubt that it will be fraught with interest. We will be watching the* Review *for later indications of your movements, upward and/or sideways. But in that climate, what will happen to mint stamps?*
> —Card of May 16, 1968

Through the years, I had bombarded him with an embarrassingly large number of requests for recommendations. Now, I had asked him for another:

> *The letter has been mailed. I hope it helps. I dislike these wide open requests for recommendation where you have to guess what they want but I suppose the checklist type is pretty useless too.*

Thanks for the invitation to stop by Huntsville. I'll fly to NY then to Luxemburg and then bus to Paris, saving the school $70 or so and costing me an extra day and two nights' sleep, but I have this old-fashioned compulsion about thrift and never having been an administrator, have never outgrown it in my limited travels.

Six months seem hardly time enough to grind through the mass of material I ought to check but I should at least touch the required bases before beginning to write. It is hard to disprove a negative, and research is the same way. You can never be sure that something does not exist and may pop up to call a question on the data you have accumulated. Well, there is no security anywhere in this world, I guess.

—Interoffice memo of February 5, 1969

Responding to grapevine accounts having to do with the college in the Southwest where I was then teaching, he chortled:

We hear strange reports . . . about the wondrous ways your educational leaders perform their wonders, as in selecting presidents for your school. We surely have our problems too, 99 percent unnecessary, but I'm not sure I'd want to trade.

—Typed letter of April 15, 1971

One of my classmates, Dr. Bruce Anderson, wrote about Utt's impact on *his* life[6]:

I realized when he died in 1985 that my file of seventy-two Utt letters was one of my most precious possessions, the

[6]*Bruce Anderson, "Not Some Saintly Mr. Chips: A Memoir of Walter Utt," Spectrum, 18, No. 4.*

kind you grab first when the house is on fire. I also recognized that outside my immediate family, this Christian teacher had been the most important person in my life.

Noting that some conservative church reactionaries considered Utt to be a cynic, Anderson countered with

At heart he was a defender of the faith—witty, skeptical, independent, but a defender nonetheless. Somebody once said that the world is divided into two camps: liberals who wonder why the world isn't better and conservatives who are surprised that it isn't worse. By that definition, Walter was a profound conservative.

All these thoughts and more sifted through the chambers of my mind during that daylong drive north to Pacific Union College. Then came the evening we all gathered in Dr. Utt's old classroom. His favorite cartoons and sayings graced the walls. Cartoons such as the one by Baloo in which one caveman solemnly informs the other, "Do you realize that there are enough rocks to kill every man, woman, and child on earth five times over?" or another by Hector Breele depicting an impoverished man and woman sitting in a bare tenement flat. The woman deadpans, "I sometimes find it hard to believe what it was like before we had nuclear power." And sayings or quotes such as:

"Stupidity is actually responsible for much of what we attribute to malice."
—Anonymous

"He leaps purposefully from fragmentary data to shaky assumption and on to firm conclusion."
—Book review in American Historical Review

"Is the world run by smart ones who are putting us on, or by imbeciles who really mean it?"
—Anonymous

"A fanatic is a person who does what God would do if He had all the facts."
—Anonymous

"The spectacle of nuts seeking rendezvous with nutcrackers is not a pageant of the past."
—Eliot Janeway

Gradually, as we chuckled at these tangible representations of his teaching life, the room filled. Some I knew from years before; many were younger than I and were unknown to me. The Utt family was there, as were a number of Utt's close friends among the faculty. Brooding over the room was an air of expectancy: *What was going to happen?*

Finally the moderator stood, welcomed us, and stated that there was no program, no agenda; the program was *us*. Whatever we cared to say about this man's life—well, here was our opportunity to do so.

There was a long silence. If my memory serves me right, I was either the first, or one of the first, to speak. I told them about all the letters and cards Dr. Utt had written to me since college, how all through the years, he had *been there* for me. In essence, I was more than a bit proud: I didn't say, but implied—*I must be someone very special.* Imagine my chagrin as I then listened to testi-monial after testimonial and discovered that I was in a *room full* of men and women Dr. Utt had cared enough about to stay in touch with, to *be there* for, through the years!

I believe that experience was one of the defining moments of my lifetime—the revelation that I was anything but unique in Dr. Utt's life—merely one of *many!* That evening represents an epiphany in my life. It was the last domino of a cascade started several years before by an adult degree student who asked me a most pointed question: "Dr. Wheeler, are you my friend just until graduation—or are you my friend for the *long haul?*" She knew I'd be there for her until graduation, for I was paid to be, but she wanted *more:* a friendship that would keep going after the money stopped. That question had gnawed at me ever since. Now, here in this old classroom was the memory of a *real* mentor, not a pale imitation of one. We are, after all, a society of throwaway relationships: *I'll be your friend for as long as the good times last, for as long as it's to my advantage to stay friends—but don't expect me to stay a moment longer!* Sadly, too many of our "friend-ships" are little better than one-night stands and are based on nothing but self-gratification.

So it was that it all came together for me: the past, the present, and the future. What was my response to be? After a great deal of soul-searching and prayer, I made a vow to God that from that day forward, the number one priority for the rest of my life would be long-term, for-life mentoring. Not just with students in formal classrooms but with *everyone* the good Lord brought into my life. So many of these relationships are short, only moments long. I may sit next to someone in a plane, a train, a restaurant, a public gathering, and most likely will never see that person again—sort of like Christ's meeting the dissolute woman of

Samaria at the well (we have no record that they ever met again). Same with the rich young ruler. Yet those two meetings have influenced men and women everywhere for almost two thousand years.

After I made that solemn vow, the Lord led me back to the formal classroom for ten more years. Then He led me out of it again into the much broader classroom represented by my books, audiotapes, and day-to-day interactions with His sheep everywhere I go.

This is perhaps the greatest legacy I received from Dr. Utt. That and his belief in me, that God had a plan for my life—a mission, if you please, a responsibility uniquely mine.

Today there is a Walter C. Utt endowed Chair of History at Pacific Union College, but the real Utt endowment is in our hearts and cannot possibly be measured in mere money.

So it is, will ever be, that the echoes of those shuffling footsteps and staccato taps of a cane daily bring home to me this message:

Life is short, life is frail, and there is no guarantee of a tomorrow. All we have is today, this moment, and the people who come our way. In the end, our money, things, houses, and land will be passed on to others. The only thing that will remain to show that we lived on this earth will be the impact of our life, acts, and words on those whose lives intersected with ours.

And, in years to come, may it be said of each of you, of me, by those who knew us and feel blessed:

"I can see him. . . ."

"I can see her. . . ."

Joe Wheeler fan? Like curling up with a good story? Try these other Joe Wheeler books that will give you that "warm all over" feeling.

HEART TO HEART STORIES OF LOVE

Remember old-fashioned romance? The hauntingly beautiful, gradual unfolding of the petals of love, leading up to the ultimate full flowering of marriage and a lifetime together? From the story of the young army lieutenant returning from World War II to meet his female pen pal at Grand Central Station in the hope that their friendship will develop into romance, to the tale of a young woman who finds love in the romantic history of her grandmother, this collection satisfies the longing for stories of genuine, beautiful, lasting love.

Heart to Heart Stories of Love will warm your heart with young love, rekindled flames, and promises kept.
0-8423-1833-X

HEART TO HEART STORIES OF FRIENDSHIP

A touching collection of timeless tales that will uplift your soul. For anyone who has ever experienced or longed for the true joy of friendship, these engaging stories are sure to inspire laughter, tears, and tender remembrances. Share them with a friend or loved one.
0-8423-0586-6

HEART TO HEART STORIES FOR DADS

This collection of classic tales is sure to tug at your heart and take up permanent residence in your memories. These stories about fathers, beloved teachers, mentors, pastors, and other father figures are suitable for reading aloud to the family or for enjoying alone for a cozy evening's entertainment.
0-8423-3634-6

HEART TO HEART STORIES FOR MOMS

This heartwarming collection includes stories about the selfless love of mothers, stepmothers, surrogate mothers, and mentors. Moms in all stages of life will cherish stories that parallel their own, those demonstrating the bond between child, mother, and grandmother. A collection to cherish for years to come.
0-8423-3603-6

HEART TO HEART STORIES FOR SISTERS

Heart to Heart Stories for Sisters is a touching collection of classic short stories that is sure to become a family favorite. These stories about sisters and the relationships that bind them together are perfect for reading aloud to the whole family, for giving to your own sister, or simply for enjoying alone.
0-8423-5378-X

HEART TO HEART STORIES FOR GRANDPARENTS

Grandparents and grandchildren share a special bond—because there's something almost magical about that relationship. From the story of a man who lovingly cares for his grandmother after she develops Alzheimer's disease, to the tale of a woman whose advice helps her great-granddaughter decide which man to marry, this beautiful volume will touch your heart and encourage you to savor the time you spend with family members—of all generations.
0-8423-5379-8

CHRISTMAS IN MY HEART
Volume IX

From the tale of the orphan boy who loses a beloved puppy but finds a loving home for Christmas, to the narrative of an entire town that gives an impoverished family an unexpectedly joyful Christmas, these heartwarming stories will touch your soul with the true spirit of the season. Featured authors include O. Henry, Grace Livingston Hill, Margaret Sangster, Jr., and others.

Christmas is a time for families to take time to sit together, perhaps around a crackling blaze in the fireplace, and reminisce about Christmases of the past. Enjoy the classic stories found in this book and understand why thousands of families have made the Christmas in My Heart series part of their traditions.
0-8423-5189-2

CHRISTMAS IN MY HEART
Volume X

Christmas in My Heart, vol. 10 will bring a tear to your eye and warmth to your heart as you read the story of a lonely little girl who helps a heartbroken mother learn to love again, or the tale of a cynical old shopkeeper who discovers the true meaning of Christmas through the gift of a crippled man. Authors include Pearl S. Buck, Harry Kroll, Margaret Sangster, Jr., and others.
0-8423-5380-1

CHRISTMAS IN MY HEART
Volume XI

The Christmas season is a time for reflection and peace, a time with family and friends. As you read the story of a father desperately searching for the perfect gift for his little girl, or the account of two brothers who learn a meaningful lesson about God's love from a pair of scrawny Christmas trees, you'll expereience anew the joys and meaning of the season.
0-8423-5626-6